Changeling Press LLC

ChangelingPress.com

Falcon/ Dominic Duet
A Bones MC Romance
Marteeka Karland

Falcon/ Dominic Duet
A Bones MC Romance
Marteeka Karland

ISBN: 978-1-60521-941-7

Publisher:
Changeling Press LLC
315 N. Centre St.
Martinsburg, WV 25404
ChangelingPress.com

Printed in the U.S.A.

Editor: Jean Cooper
Cover Artist: Marteeka Karland

The individual stories in this anthology have been previously released in E-Book format.

Table of Contents

Falcon (Grim Road MC 7)
A Bones MC Romance
Marteeka Karland

It's all fun and games until my ex shows up from the dead.

Gina: For over a year I've lived in fear, a monster terrorizing me within the gates of the Grim Road MC compound. The club took care of the physical problem, but demons still ride me hard. Although I've learned to trust the people I interact with on a daily basis, I'm still too anxious to explore the compound unless I'm with one of the old ladies or Lemon. Or Falcon... He always seems to be there when the fear threatens to swallow me whole. He's protective and caring, and he takes me for rides on his Harley. Which he had painted pink because he found out I wanted to ride a pink bike. How many men in a motorcycle club did that?

Falcon: What happened to Gina at the hands of Grim Road, myself included, is something that will haunt me for the rest of my life. My only chance at redemption is to help her heal and feel safe again. I'm too old for her, but I can't seem to care. I want to protect her, but I'm watching her to an unhealthy degree, waiting for the next time she needs someone to bring her back to reality and assure her she's safe. Until the day she invites me inside her sanctuary without a chaperone. I'd never take advantage of Gina. Not intentionally. Then again, I never expected my ex-fiancée to come back from the dead.

Chapter One

Falcon

The soft cry coming from Gina's bedroom window damned near broke my heart. She did fine most days, when she had the girls to distract her. But at night, when she was alone in that house, nightmares visited her regularly. Those nightmares were partly my fault and that was why I couldn't let go of this need to see she was safe. Which is why I was currently sitting underneath her open window outside her house. At one in the morning.

Yeah. That wasn't creepy or anything. Thank God she still stayed in the compound. I knew she wasn't really comfortable here, but she had nowhere else to go. Though she typically stayed in her house or in the fenced-in backyard, she would very occasionally leave the compound to grocery shop or whatever. She *never* went anywhere inside the compound by herself other than to drive from her house to the main gate and back.

Another soft cry followed by a small sob echoed in the night. It was a scared, lonely sound, much like that of a child lost from its parents in a crowd. Among the myriad night noises in the wildlife reserve where our compound was nestled, she sounded like a caged animal too scared to fight.

With a shake of my head, I dug my phone out from my back pocket and moved away from the window slightly behind a shrub and called her. When I heard her phone play a trilling notification, I moved farther away so she couldn't hear me speaking through her open window. She answered on the fourth ring.

"H-hello?"

"Hey, Gina. I hope I didn't wake you up."

"I -- no. You didn't. Falcon?"

"Yeah. Probably shoulda led with that, huh?" I tried to make fun of myself to distract her. I knew from months of watching over her and listening to her nightmares she was always shaken when she woke.

"Sorry. I should have checked to see who was calling before I answered." She sounded a little more awake and even managed a small laugh.

"I'm really sorry. I thought I saw your light on and thought something might be wrong. About the time you answered, I realized it was Rocket and Lemon's place."

There was a short pause and I thought I heard her shuffling around. Maybe sliding the covers from her body so she could sit on the edge of the bed. And, Goddamn, that image needed to stay the fuck outta my head!

"You were... checking on me?"

"Well, yeah." I hoped I sounded sheepish and embarrassed but I wasn't that great an actor. But if it pulled her out of her nightmares, I'd suffer through it. Gladly. "I guess I was."

She took in a shuddering breath before speaking again. "Because of what happened?"

I had to be careful about my answer here. I didn't want her thinking I felt obligated to look after her, but I didn't want to scare her either. God knew she had plenty of reasons to be scared of me.

"Because you need someone looking after you and I kind of enjoy the job."

"You don't have to, you know. I'll be fine."

"I know you will. You're strong. You need time to heal and to learn to trust yourself again."

"I didn't expect you to say that."

"Why not? What should I have said?" I kept my

voice neutral and conversational. I wanted her to keep talking so she could settle her mind. I always managed to find a way to get through to her when she had a nightmare. I don't know if she suspected I was watching her or not, but whenever I'd hear her crying or calling out in fear, I'd send a text. Or knock on her door. Or call. If she'd noticed the timing, she hadn't said anything. Positive or negative.

"I thought you'd tell me I'd have to learn to trust you. Why would you think I didn't trust myself?"

I had to smile. I'd led her straight where I wanted her to go and she'd done so without hesitation. "Because you already trust everyone in this club. What you don't trust is your own judgment telling you to trust us."

She was silent so long I thought I might have overplayed my hand. Then her soft voice asked, "How do you know I trust you?"

"Because, when Rocket and Lemon said the club would pay for a place outside the compound if you wanted to get away from us, you declined."

"Yeah," she said on a sigh. "I suppose you're right. I just couldn't stand the thought of being out on my own again. I was obviously not very good on my own the first time."

"That wasn't your fault, Gina. Once he got you back here, it was easy for him to make you feel like you didn't have a choice. You know better now and you *choose* to stay."

"I never really thought about it that way. I couldn't get past having to be on my own. And Lemon... well..."

"What about her? You know she's solidly in your corner. Right?"

"That's just it, Falcon. I *do* know. She didn't make

excuses for anyone. She didn't doubt anything I told her. She believed everything and I was quick to tell her you guys thought I was willing when... you know... when you..." Even now she couldn't say it, and I wanted to claw out my own heart.

"Yeah, honey. I know. We're all ashamed of that, even if we didn't know. We could have taken the time to talk to you more. Or at all, really." I gave a self-deprecating snort of laughter. "More importantly, we could have made sure you knew you weren't in danger from any of us. All you had to do was tell someone you wanted away from Hammer and we'd have removed you from the situation and asked questions later. We didn't make it clear so that's on us."

"I guess," she said softly. "Seems like both of us were victims of Hammer's deception."

"I'd say that's a fair statement."

I heard sounds on her end as she moved from her bedroom. I heard a door open, then close. Moments later, the light in her living room came on.

"You said you saw a light. That you thought it was mine." She sounded better now. More herself. Though I hated that she'd donned the air of indifference she hid behind, I was glad that, at least subconsciously, she'd trusted me enough to tell me what she had.

"Yeah. I did."

"Are you close by, then?"

"Yeah. Just outside." Not a lie.

"Um, would you, uh..." She cleared her throat. "Would you like some coffee?"

"You good with me being in your space without one of the women nearby?"

"I think so." Her voice said she was trying to convince herself she could do this and wasn't doing a very good job. "You'd leave if I got overwhelmed. Right?"

"Absolutely. In fact, why don't we sit outside on the porch? That way you can keep the door between us if you want to."

There was a pause, then a sniffle before she spoke again. "You'd do that? Just to make sure I was comfortable?"

"Gina, honey. Of course. I like bein' around you. I like talkin' to you and just wavin' at you as I drive by. I'll do whatever it takes to make sure you always want to spend that kind of time with me." God, could I sound any more pathetic? Did I fucking care?

"Come over, Falcon. I've unlocked the door and am making coffee. Let yourself in. We can sit and chat for a while."

"You don't have to tell me twice, honey."

I chuckled as I took my time walking up her driveway. I knocked loudly before opening the door. Even though she was expecting me, I wanted to make sure she was well aware of where I was in her home.

"Hey." Her smile was small, but so beautiful it made my heart ache. How anyone could have hurt this woman was beyond me. She carried a tray with two mugs, a pot of black coffee, cream and sugar. That was something else about Gina. She was always prepared with a way to entertain guests. I got the feeling at least some of that came from the need to have something to concentrate on besides being scared all the time. The other was a desire to make people comfortable and welcome. The way she dealt with all the children the club had recently acquired seemed to fulfill that side of her as well. Which gave her an added distraction from her fear. "I have some caramel sauce in the fridge if you'd rather."

"Black's fine for me. Thank you, Gina."

She fixed hers with a liberal amount of cream and sugar before blowing gently over the liquid and taking a careful sip. I watched her as I took a sip of my own coffee, letting the silence stretch. I'd follow her lead.

"Um, I should thank you. I actually had dozed off and was having a nightmare when you called." One hand cupped her mug while she ran her other hand up and down her arm.

It surprised me she admitted that so easily. I thought it was probably good though. Like she was really trying to give me the benefit of the doubt and take me at my word that I wanted to look out for her.

"In that case, I'm glad I didn't hang up the second I realized it was Rocket and Lemon's house I was seeing with a light on."

Again, she gave me a small smile. This time I thought she looked more relaxed. She was still on guard, but she was at least somewhat comfortable.

"Can I ask you a question?" A light blush dusted her cheeks, and she couldn't meet my gaze. Her breathing became more rapid and she fiddled with the coffee mug in her hand.

"Of course. Anything."

She swallowed, obviously nervous but determined to plow on. "Why do you keep taking me for rides on that pink bike?"

I let out a surprised chuckle, not able to help the burst of mirth. Lemon, the bitch, had painted my Harley pink because she said Gina had always wanted a pink bike. So Lemon had made it happen. But she'd told Gina I'd insisted she do it because I wanted to make things right with her. Lemon had told me I could thank her later. I suppose now was later.

"You don't like it? I mean, I can stop --"

"No!" She interrupted, reaching out to grip my wrist firmly, like she was trying to prevent me from doing anything drastic. I had to grin because I knew there was no way she wanted me to stop taking her on those rides. "I love it! I cried the first day you pulled up on it and told me we were going to take a spin around the compound. I know the guys give you shit about it, but you haven't had it repainted or traded it off. I just wondered, you know…" She pulled her hand away from my arm and I felt the loss. I liked that she'd kept the contact as long as she had. "Why would you keep riding with me on it when you hate the color?"

This, I had an answer for. I reached out slowly, giving her time to pull back if she didn't want my touch. She turned her hand over, and I laced my fingers through hers lightly. "Because you cried the first day I pulled up and told you we were goin' on a ride."

She sucked in a breath and her eyes got glassy with tears. I gave her what I was sure was a thunderous look, but honestly, I couldn't help it. I panicked! "Don't you dare cry on me."

Thankfully, she must have seen the humor in the situation because she laughed through her tears. "I never knew such hard men could be so affected by a girl's tears. I mean, I thought you guys weren't exactly sympathetic types, but I'm beginning to think otherwise. I've noticed that if one of the old ladies so much as has a lower lip start quivering, you go rounding up the wagons and calling in reinforcements to make the tears stop." She shook her head even as she smiled and used her free hand to wipe at her eyes with a napkin. "It's not natural."

I chuckled, relief flooding me I'd managed to

stave off those fucking tears. "I agree, honey. It ain't natural. But our women seemed to have done that to us. And you know what else?" When she smiled and shook her head like she couldn't wait to hear this, I continued, "We love every fuckin' second of it, and I could give a good Goddamn if everyone in the club knows how we feel."

Chapter Two

Gina

When I first came to Grim Road, I thought I'd found a paradise. It hadn't taken long for Hammer to make me realize how wrong I'd been. I thought he loved me or I'd never have come here with him. I still don't know why he wanted me at the compound. There were women here who would let him do whatever he wanted to them. Well, within reason. I'd heard the women discussing some of the guys and knew they all believed they had protection if anyone got too rough.

Now, I knew the girls were right. I'd also found out Hammer was the exception rather than the norm. It took me a long while -- and constant reassurance by Lemon -- to get to a place where I felt comfortable with the guys here. I still wasn't comfortable with everyone. It was hard to look them in the face after Hammer had basically whored me out to them all.

I knew the guys wouldn't hurt me now. When Hammer had me under his control, he had me convinced his brothers in this MC would make me wish I was dead if I ever went against him. Grim Road's compound was hidden in a wildlife reserve. I had no idea how they'd managed that, but I was smart enough to know if this place was a secret, they wouldn't let me leave alive.

Lemon had told me I could go if I wanted and she'd make sure I had a place to live but I was reluctant to leave Grim Road. Yes, I'd been terrorized for a year and a half, but I truly understood the difference between Hammer and the other guys in Grim I'd met. When Hammer took me, I had nothing. No one. I'd been living on the street. At Grim Road, now that they realized I hadn't been here willingly, I had someone looking after me. Several someones. Falcon hadn't been the only one to take me on a bike ride, but he was the one who was still around. He was the one who always came around to check on me or make me get out of the house into the fresh air.

And I liked the way he smiled at me.

"I know it's late, but do you want to go on a ride?" He still held my hand and I found I didn't want him to let go just yet. I had to smile. The guy didn't act like a badass biker or military guy. He acted like a teenager with a crush. It was one of the things I liked most about him.

"Um, we could just sit here."

He gave me a puzzled look, then glanced down at our entwined fingers like he was just noticing. I thought he might pull away, but he didn't. His fingers closed even tighter around my hand and he smiled. "We can sit here as long as you want."

That was the thing about Falcon. He and Lemon bickered back and forth like competitive siblings, but with me, Falcon was always so patient. He was around me all the time. Not a day went by I didn't either see him or talk to him. We'd had sex. You know. Before. When Hammer had given his OK for the guys to have me if they wanted me. I'd fucked him the same as I had a lot of his brothers. Since he found out I hadn't been as willing as he'd thought, Falcon had never once touched me in a sexual way. He'd protected my personal space and always made sure I knew I could depend on him if I needed anything. All of our interactions were as platonic as it got and that gave me the courage to enjoy our time together. Falcon was with me because he wanted to be. Not because he thought I'd fuck him, or for any other self-serving reason. He just liked being with me.

"Want to watch a movie?" He jerked his head at the TV. "I got all kinds of streaming services we can log into."

I squeezed his hand briefly before tugging away. "You don't have to stay with me, you know."

"Yeah. I know." He grinned before standing and reaching for me to pull me to my feet. "Now. I gave you your chance to pick a movie. It's my turn. Go make me some popcorn and I'll pick the movie."

I couldn't help the surprised giggle that escaped my mouth. Falcon winked at me before going to the living room to find his movie. Falcon and I ate a lot of popcorn. Popping a batch wasn't difficult and didn't take much time. I popped two batches. His with salt. Mine with popcorn butter and kettle corn seasoning. I brought us both sodas.

As always, Falcon sat on one end of the couch, one ankle crossed over the opposite knee and his arm over the back of the seat next to him. He sat first, not to claim a spot on my furniture, but to give me the choice to sit on the opposite end or next to him. Usually, I'd start on the side away from him. By the end of whatever we were watching at the time, I'd be sitting next to him. That was as far as I'd been brave enough to go.

Tonight, I sat next to him. I leaned against him and he let his fingers play along my shoulder. He didn't pull me against him or try to wrap his arm around me. He just let me know his hand was there.

I took a deep breath, closing my eyes and letting his scent fill me. The heat from his body filled me with warmth and I wanted to curl up in his lap and have his arms wrapped tightly around me, just for the sensation. The closeness. I craved that closeness, was starved for it. But other than a few of the women, I didn't like being touched. I wasn't a hugger. The only person I had any desire to have wrap their arms around me was Falcon.

We sat in silence, eating popcorn and watching *The Fifth Element*. And yes. It was my favorite movie which Falcon knew.

"Thank you." My words were barely above a whisper, but I knew Falcon would hear me. He always heard me.

"For what, honey?"

"For sitting up with me. For watching out for me. I know you're keeping a closer eye on me than I should be comfortable with, but you make me feel safe. I never thought I'd have that in my life. So, yeah, I know you waking me up from my nightmares isn't a coincidence. I just don't care. Thank you, Falcon. For all of it."

Falcon grunted before leaning down to brush a kiss on the top of my head. We sat in silence for a while before he said, "So… You're saying you don't mind that I was stalking you. Right?"

I couldn't help the laughter bubbling up from inside me. I turned my face into his chest, clinging to his shirt as I shook with silent laughter.

"Don't see nothin' so funny 'bout that," he grumbled, but I noticed how he threaded his fingers through my hair and massaged my scalp lightly. "Just wanted to make sure we were, you know, on the same page."

"Yes, Falcon. We're on the same page. I'm not mad that you were stalking me." I smiled up at him, an invitation I hadn't really meant to make, but now that I'd offered, I wasn't backing down.

The relaxed grin on Falcon's face faded slightly. He held my gaze, looking for something. "If you don't want me to kiss you, Gina, tell me now." I swallowed, but my focus fell onto his lips. Mine parted and I sucked in a ragged breath.

"Good." Slowly, Falcon moved closer to brush his lips with mine. They were warm and firm. Commanding yet not overwhelming or rough. He licked the seam of my lips lightly but didn't push even when I opened my mouth.

The kiss didn't last long. Seconds. But when he pulled back to look down at me, I felt like I was high. My head spun and my entire being was focused on where our lips had touched. I whimpered and almost chased him, needing to get his lips back on mine. Falcon's fingers gently brushing my cheek stopped me.

"Thank you for the kiss, Gina."

"I liked it." I ducked my head, embarrassed.

"I didn't scare you?"

My reflex was to answer with an immediate "no." But I wanted to be honest with Falcon. While everyone in Grim Road had been good to me, Falcon had gone above and beyond. And I genuinely liked the guy, not to mention that I wasn't too proud to admit I was sexually attracted to him. I probably shouldn't be. I was sure a psychiatrist would have a field day with me, but I *was* attracted to him. Not to anyone else I'd interacted with. Only Falcon.

I stared up at him, my lips still tingling from his kiss. "No."

He gave me a quizzical look. "You thought about your answer. Are you sure? Last thing I want is for you to ever be scared of me, Gina."

"That's why I thought about what you asked. I'm scared of everything. But I'm not scared of you, Falcon. Not at all."

I thought he might kiss me again -- wanted him

to kiss me again -- but I also wasn't as honest with myself as I tried to be with him. Even though I wanted his kiss again, I was also still emotionally tapped from the nightmare that woke me up initially. Instead, he kissed my forehead and urged me closer to him before putting his arm back on the couch and letting his fingers rest on my shoulder again.

I took a breath. Then another. The longer I sat there with Falcon, the more I relaxed. I hadn't realized how tense I'd become. Probably because that was my default setting since Hammer had brought me here. Even knowing I was safe, sometimes I just couldn't get over that feeling of wondering if someone was going to walk through the door of my house and want something from me I wasn't willing to give. Should I have left after Hammer died a few months ago? Probably. But I was glad I'd stayed. My story wasn't a pretty happy ever after, but I thought I could be happy. I just needed to get past what had happened and let myself realize that part was over. The people here were good people. I'd just managed to stumble onto a bad apple.

We sat on the couch and neither of us moved. It was like an uneasy truce between us. As long as neither of us moved, everything would be OK. I could pretend Falcon was mine and he could pretend our past had been different. Both fantasies were fiction. It was a depressing thought.

Little by little, I relaxed. I had my head on his shoulder. Occasionally, Falcon would nuzzle my head. We didn't talk. We didn't move. We simply watched the movie. Our popcorn sat on the coffee table along with our drinks, untouched. I had the odd thought that I'd wasted the popcorn I'd made earlier, but it was more something that caught my attention and tugged at me, keeping me from dozing off when I started to drift. Not that it helped.

The next thing I remember was being laid carefully in my bed. Someone pulled up the covers and tucked me in. Then I opened my eyes just as Falcon kissed my forehead while he stroked a few stray curls from my face.

"Sleep well, baby. If anyone deserves a good night's rest, you do."

"Falcon?" I gazed up at him, my eyes blurry as I tried to keep them open when they were so heavy.

"I'm here, honey. Ain't goin' nowhere." His voice was husky but gentle and soft. He reached out to turn off the bedside lamp and the room was enveloped in darkness.

"You can stay if you don't want to go home so late," I managed. I was so tired my words were slurring.

"I'm stayin'," he said, still stroking my hair in soothing movements of his hand. "I'll be here if you need me. You're not alone, Gina. I'm your protector. Always remember that."

I blinked up at him, sleep already starting to claim me again. "Do you promise?"

"On my life, baby. Anyone who ever tries to hurt you again, I'll kill 'em myself. No matter who it is. Even me." His words should have unsettled me. There was so much to unwrap in that simple declaration. Instead, my entire body relaxed, almost like when alcohol starts to hit after you've already done a couple more shots than you probably should have. I nodded my head and smiled up at him. "OK." It was the last thing I remember before sleep took me.

Chapter Three

Falcon

I needed to go home. Needed to get out of this place before I did something stupid. Like crawl in the bed with the broken little doll and hold her until the pieces fused back together. Gina was quite possibly the strongest person I'd ever met. Even stronger than Lemon, who regularly busted my balls.

This woman chose to stay in a place where she'd been terrorized for over a year. I get she'd had a shit life even before she came here, but I was surprised when she didn't head out of the compound like the hounds of hell were after her once she knew she was free to leave.

My phone buzzed in my back pocket. I pulled it out and checked the message and nearly growled when I saw Dom's name. I'd known this was coming, but I hadn't anticipated that I'd be in Gina's house with her most of the night. The need to tell him to fuck the hell off was making my jaw clench. Yeah. Not the best idea, especially since I hadn't been a patched member of Grim Road long enough to go against the sergeant at arms. Which… yeah. I wasn't a pussy by any means, but going against Dom without a better reason than, "I'm watching my woman sleep. Piss off," would be stupid.

Dom: *Need you at the clubhouse.*
Me: *Sunrise.*
Dom: *Now.*

Fuck. I stood and pulled the quilt higher on her shoulder before leaving the room. I locked her door when I left the house. Leaving was so hard it was a physical ache in my chest. It felt wrong because I knew anything I'd managed to forge over the last several months could easily be undone if I disappeared on her now.

I hurried to my bike, which I'd parked in Rocket's driveway when I'd gone to stand vigil. Rocket and Lemon both knew I did this, but neither had said a word about it to anyone, including me. I figured, by parking there on the regular, if Rocket or Lemon wanted to warn me off Gina, they would.

The ride to the main clubhouse took less than five minutes. I lined up with the other bikes in the lot before striding inside. The club members present sat at the various tables in groups, talking among themselves. A few nursed their beer, but most were quietly waiting for the meeting to start.

"Nice of you to join us, Falcon." Dom crossed his arms over his chest while Ringo, the enforcer for Grim Road, gave me a knowing smirk. Yeah. They all knew what I was doing. Some approved, but there were a couple who were pretty pissed about it because they thought she needed to get away from all of us. Even if she didn't want to.

"Bite me," I shot back automatically. It got a few chuckles. Except for Dom.

The bigger man pointed his finger at me and raised an eyebrow. "I will beat your ass, you little punk." Which got even more chuckles.

"All right, all right." Rocket stood and got to business. "We got a heads-up from a paramilitary company called ExFil. Most of you know the place and the guy who owns it. His name's Joe Gill. Used to be president of a club in Somerset, Kentucky called Bones MC."

"Most of the guys at Salvation's Bane MC work for 'em too, right?" Jackhammer was a newer guy. He hadn't started out as a prospect, like most of us. He'd been brought in as a favor to Boon. Boon had been in Grim Road the longest of anyone in the club. He was blunt and to the point and didn't care who the fuck he offended. All traits Jackhammer tried to imitate. Only problem was, Jackhammer wasn't Boon.

"They are." Rocket glared at Jackhammer, no doubt knowing the other man was about to protest.

"Then what the fuck do they need us for?" Jackhammer snorted a laugh, like he'd gotten one over on… someone? Salvation's Bane maybe? The man was as mean as he was stupid. I honestly had no idea what his thought processes were and had no desire to find out. I also think Boon was suckin' some serious dick to get this dumb shit into Grim Road. We had all been black ops at one point in our service. Most of us had either outlived our usefulness or were on a government kill list somewhere. Not Jackhammer. He'd been good for a while, but once he decided to show his ass, he tended to go big.

Rocket's jaw clenched. Yeah. I wasn't the only one who hated the little bastard. "Did I say they asked for help?"

"That's where you were goin'." Jackhammer stood, moving a couple steps in Rocket's direction. "Tell me I'm wrong." He stuck his chin out, directly challenging Rocket.

"Fucker has a death wish," I muttered, shaking my head. I covered my mouth with my hand in case I burst out laughing when Lemon castrated the bastard in a few seconds. Last thing I wanted was for Lemon to think I was on her side in anything.

"Yep." Rattler had been my best friend for as long as I could remember. We'd grown up together, gone to the Marines together, then joined covert ops together. Which is how we'd ended up here together.

"Ten bucks on Lemon," I said softly.

"You've lost your Goddamn mind if you think I'm lettin' you tell Lemon I bet against her," Rattler grumbled.

Around us, similar conversations hummed softly. Dom scowled at us. Then pulled a folded bill from his pocket and said something to Ringo and shoved the money at him. Ringo held up his hands and backed away, shaking his head. Obviously, Ringo was smarter than he looked.

As if on cue, Lemon sauntered from where she'd been fiddling with the big dartboard on the wall behind Rocket. Before I realized what she was gonna do, Lemon marched straight up to Jackhammer. When she got close, she put one dart in her teeth sideways, like a pencil, then stabbed the other two into Jackhammer's thighs. The third she saved for his crotch.

A collective "OHHHH!" went up around the room before everyone laughed. Everyone except Rocket. No one offered to help Jackhammer.

Rocket let the ruckus continue for a couple of minutes before quieting everyone with a look. "What I said, you dumbshit, is they gave us a heads-up."

Jackhammer was on his knees on the floor of the clubhouse. He looked around the room until he caught Boon's gaze. "Ain't you gonna help me?"

Boon gave him a disgusted look. "Shoulda *helped you* permanently the last time you asked me that fuckin' question. Instead, I brought you here. To my home." Boon leaned back in his chair and propped his feet on the table in front of him. "Apparently you still ain't grasped the concept of actions and consequences."

Blood was beginning to pool beneath and around

Jackhammer. Usually this was the point where Rocket scolded Lemon, and Lemon pouted and pretended to be all innocent and shit before she launched that last dart straight into Jackhammer's eye. Instead, the little hellion just stood there, twirling the point of the dart against her index finger lazily.

"You gonna get up and join the meetin' or sit there and bleed?" Rocket gave Jackhammer a look that had been known to leave prospects quaking in their boots.

With his defenses down -- because of a dart to the dick -- Jackhammer had no hope of holding his ground. He grunted and tried to rise to his feet but the darts in his thighs must have protested, because the man gave a sharp yelp.

"Jesus Christ," Boon muttered, scrubbing his hand over his eyes. "Will someone just shoot him and put him outta his misery?"

"Kinda feels a little like shootin' a helpless, if stupid, teenager." Ringo took out his sidearm and chambered a round. "But I can sure the fuck do it."

"Oh, for fuck's sake." Finally! Lemon pushed her way past Rocket and knelt in front of Jackhammer. Before he knew what Lemon was doing, she reached out and yanked both darts from Jackhammer's legs. Which caused another yelp. That yelp turned into a full-on girl scream when she yanked the dart from his crotch. "There. All better! Go see Bullet for a tetanus shot later."

"You fuckin' bitch!" Jackhammer screamed. "I'll fuckin' kill you for this! Fuckin' whore!"

I stood so fast, my chair tumbled back. I wasn't the only one. None of us were as fast as Rocket, though. He pulled his gun and shot Jackhammer in the crotch. Not once. Three. Fucking. Times.

"You want somethin' to scream about, you pissant little motherfucker?" Rocket shot him in the crotch a fourth time. "Try that." Again, Rocket shot. "How about that, too?" Blood was now everywhere. Jackhammer was covered in it and there was no doubt Rocket had hit one or both femoral arteries. Probably every blood vessel in Jackhammer's pelvis. In any event, Jackhammer was no longer screaming. It wasn't like Rocket to lose his cool, and definitely not like him to kill indiscriminately. Which told me Jackhammer had been way more trouble than Rocket was willing to take.

'Course, it coulda just been the fact the fool had threatened to kill Lemon, no matter how much pain the fucker was in at her doing. The easiest way to unleash the outlaw in Rocket was to threaten his woman. Lemon had had a couple close calls since she met Rocket and the president hadn't gotten over any of it yet. None of us had.

"Thank Christ." Boon holstered his own gun before sitting back down. "I'd hate to've had to explain to Bessy how I'd killed her fuckin' kid when I finally got to hell."

"Jackhammer was your stepson?" I asked before I could stop myself and immediately winced. "Never mind. Ain't my business."

Boon gave me an impatient look. "Hell no, the bastard ain't my stepson. He was my old lady's kid. I never claimed him in any way, shape, or form." He spat where Jackhammer lay in a heap on the floor nearby. "Told you this was your last chance to straighten up, kid. Shoulda fuckin' listened."

"Can we get on with this or would someone else like to die?" The look on Rocket's face said he'd had enough.

Scrub, the cleaner for Grim Road, stood and nudged Jackhammer's lifeless form with the toe of his boot. When the other man didn't move, Scrub shrugged. "I'll take him out back to dispose of. Let me know when the meeting's over, and I'll see what I need to do here."

Rocket just grunted before continuing. "Ain't no easy way to say this. Rattler. Falcon. One member of your team survived your last mission. She's alive, but a prisoner."

I felt like I'd been sucker punched. I think I actually grunted. "No," I whispered. "Not possible." I turned to look at Rattler who had an equally sick look on his face. Not that we valued female lives over male lives, but I hadn't missed the fact Rocket had said "she" and there was no way Rattler missed it either. "We *visually accounted for* every single man and woman in our mission. We didn't leave anyone behind, least of all a woman. Christ, Rocket!"

"I have no doubt your count was correct." Rocket dug out a thumb drive from his pocket and tossed it to me. I caught it reflexively or it would have bounced off my chest and hit the floor. I was still trying to wrap my head around what he'd said.

"We brought every one of our team back with us. They were dead, but we brought them home. We carried their bodies to the landing zone and loaded them into the aircraft ourselves." I could barely form words. Reliving the worst day in my life... Thinking about the events of that day made me nauseous. It wasn't just a matter of getting our brothers and sisters to the LZ and in the chopper. We'd had to pick up as many pieces of them as we could. In some cases, it had probably been left up to investigators to figure out what body went with that limb. Or head.

"You did. What you didn't know was there was someone on the inside of that terror cell already, giving your handler real time data. No one bothered to tell you because..." Rocket trailed off, clenching his jaw. He actually glanced over to Lemon who was focused squarely on our president. Her husband. She was as stony-faced as Rocket and, in some ways, infinitely more terrifying, even if she was still practically a fucking teenager. She nodded her head slightly and Rocket continued. "Because the operative imbedded in that shit hole was Joilyn Graves."

Instantly, Rattler got to his feet. He pulled his gun and aimed it at Rocket's head. I'll admit, I had to stop myself from doing the same. It wasn't every day someone told you a woman you thought had been dead for years had been the deep operative on your mission. And you'd left her there. Also, it probably didn't help the fact that Joilyn Graves happened to be Rattler's sister.

To the president's credit, he didn't flinch. In fact, Rocket looked like he'd been expecting exactly this reaction.

"Easy, Rattler," I said, putting my hand on his shoulder, trying to urge him to lower his weapon before he got himself -- and me -- killed. "We'll figure this out."

"You don't get to utter her name, Rocket. Not like this." I'd never seen this side of Rattler. The battle-hardened man's hand actually shook as he held his gun. "Joi died a year before everything that happened that night. You go back to ExFil or Cain or whoever the fuck told you this fuckin' horse shit and tell 'em I'm comin' to kill them."

"It's all on the flash drive, Rattler. Information that will explain everything. Obviously, the CIA didn't offer any of this. Data and his wife, Zora, along with Cain's daughter, Suzie, found this. I'm certain their means of procurement were less than legal."

Yeah. The full impact of this would hit me later, but I had bigger things to worry about right now. "You said they were givin' us a heads-up," I said after clearing my throat. Rocket had hit me with way too fucking much in way too fucking short a time for me to process. "They offerin' to let us in on this?"

Rocket nodded. "They are. Cain said he thought the two of you needed the option to go with them or not. Piston said to consider it the first official act of the South Eastern MC Alliance."

"That op went to shit two fuckin' years ago," Rattler bit out. He'd holstered his weapon, but he was still standing and looking like he wanted to be anywhere but in this fucking meeting. "What happened for ExFil to get this now?"

"Not sure," Rocket admitted. "But I think Mama and Pops might have had something to do with it. Them, or someone they know."

"What makes you say that?"

"Just something Cain said. He mentioned Pops in the same breath he told me they were being sent after your sister. That man doesn't give out information without a reason."

"When do we leave?" Rattler clenched and unclenched his fists. I knew how he felt. It had taken me a long while to make my peace with Joilyn's death. She'd died in a fiery car crash on a rural road. By the time emergency services got there, she'd been almost completely burned. The autopsy had identified her by dental records and me and Rattler had mourned her death.

Joilyn had been Rattler's last living relative. He,

Joilyn, and I had become a small family of our own. I was included with them because their parents had fostered me. I'd been orphaned when I was only eight, and Rattler and I had been best friends from the first evening I arrived at his home. Joilyn had been born three months after I arrived so I'd known her her entire life. It had devastated me and Rattler both when she'd been killed.

Now, to know she was inside that hellhole, providing us intel at risk to her life and, not only had we not known, but we'd cut and run, it felt like the absolute worst betrayal. We'd left her to her fate. Once again, I'd failed someone who depended on me. Seemed all I did was fail people. At least, it felt like I had from that night on. Even now, I was actually planning on letting down one of the most important people in my life. Leaving on this mission and leaving Gina here was going to be hard on her. But I couldn't leave Rattler to do this on his own. For more than one reason.

"You leave here in two days. Cain said he was sending a team to pick you up."

"Sounds like you expected we'd not only accept their invitation, but that we'd insist on going." I gripped Rattler's shoulder as I spoke. It looked like a show of support, but if I touched him, I could tell how tense he was. Pulling the gun on Rocket had been bad. I thought Rattler had himself back under control, but the last thing I wanted was for him to accidentally hurt someone because he wasn't thinking clearly. The PTSD resulting from that night wasn't subtle. Rattler's muscles were tight, but the trembling seemed to have stopped.

"I'm not a dumbass, Falcon." Rocket gave me an annoyed look.

"Wait." Dom looked from me and Rattler to Rocket and back. "Why would Cain make that kind of an offer? Seems risky puttin' an unknown element with a team right before going on a mission."

"It is." Rocket's gaze never left mine. "Which is why I want to know why he included you, Falcon. Rattler I get. Joilyn is his sister."

"Yeah." I scrubbed a hand over my face. I inhaled a shaky breath. "Joilyn was going to be my wife."

Chapter Four

Gina

I woke when the bed dipped and someone brushed hair off my forehead. Gentle fingers traced my cheek and chin almost reverently.

"Hey, sweetheart."

I opened my eyes and smiled up at Falcon. "Hey, yourself."

"How you feelin'?"

"Little strung out. You know. Like I didn't get much sleep." He smiled tenderly at me, but there was something in his expression I couldn't figure out. "Is everything all right?"

Falcon glanced away before shaking his head slightly. "I have to leave in a couple days, Gina. I hope I won't be gone long."

Everything inside me rebelled. I shook my head before I could stop myself. Then I closed my eyes and swallowed, trying to rid myself of the lump forming in my throat.

I sat up, pushing myself back against the headboard and tucked my knees to my chest. "Of course. Just be careful."

Falcon hesitated a moment before reaching out to carefully take my hand and I let him. "It's early. How about I fix us some breakfast and we can talk."

Something about the way he spoke set off alarm bells inside my head. "What's wrong?"

He gave me a small smile. "We can talk after we eat, baby. Everything will be fine."

"The only time people say that is when everything isn't fine." I should have known this thing with Falcon was too good to be true. I'd deluded myself into thinking we could have some kind of relationship where I wasn't a whore or someone to share with his brothers whenever he wanted a thrill.

Lord knew I'd overheard several of the club girls comment how they knew none of the patched members would ever take an old lady from the pool of club whores. Made sense, I guess. I doubted it would be comfortable if you had a woman every other man in the place had been with. Which is why I should have known better than to get my hopes up that Falcon saw me as something different.

"That's why we need to talk. So you know the whole story. Or at least as much as I know." He very slowly brought my hand to his mouth and kissed my fingers tenderly. "Don't give up on me, Gina. Please." His voice was tender and full of emotion. That was the only reason I was able to nod.

I was still dressed in the leggings and oversized T-shirt I'd had on the night before. "I probably smell gross. I should change clothes."

"You smell incredible, baby. Nothin' trumps the smell of warm woman after she's woken from a contented sleep." He smiled warmly at me. "But you do what makes you comfortable." He stood but kept my hand which meant I either had to tug away from him or get out of bed. I didn't have the strength for the latter so I followed where he led.

"I make a mean omelet." Falcon grinned at me. "Any requests?"

I gave him a small smile. "You know what I like."

"Yeah." He gave me an arrogant lift of his chin. "I do."

A few minutes later, we each had a plate full of fluffy omelet covered in cheese. Just the way I liked it. Basically, egg and cheese. What's not to like? It also meant this conversation was going to be as bad as I'd feared because Falcon didn't try to get me to have anything other than the eggs. He usually put all kinds of other shit in it. Veggies or meats. Today, though. Just an incredibly fluffy egg and cheese.

We ate in silence. Well, we pushed food around on the plate. I'm not sure either of us actually ate anything.

Finally, Falcon moved his plate away. I did the same. It was a lost cause anyway.

"Just say it," I whispered, not looking at Falcon. I knew in my heart whatever he was going to say would change our relationship. He was probably tired of having to tiptoe around me. The mere fact he'd been watching me this whole time and hadn't approached me before now told me he was probably trying to decide if he wanted to get to know me better. Or if he could approach me for sex again. Maybe that was it.

"If you want sex, all you have to do is ask. I know you'd never hurt me." I spoke softly, unable to look at Falcon. I couldn't look at him told me I wasn't ready for intimacy with him. Or maybe I was ashamed because Falcon thought he couldn't treat me like a normal woman.

"Baby." He took my hand and moved to kneel in front of me. As I looked down at him, I tried my best to fight back tears. He didn't need another round of tears or weakness on my part.

"Whatever it is you have to tell me, Falcon, just say it. I can take it."

"Let's clear some things up first, OK?" There was an intense light in his eyes. Whatever he was about to say, he felt passionately about. "*If* we ever have sex, Gina, it will be when *you're* ready. You ever don't feel comfortable with what we're doing or where we're headed, you tell me." He reached up to frame my face with his hands. "I never want you to feel like you *have* to do something you don't want to, Gina."

"But… if it's not that, are you leaving because of me?"

"No, honey." He took a breath. "My past is murky. Before I came to Grim Road, I let a lot of people down and they died. Before that, it was me and Rattler and his sister, Joilyn." He winced as he said the other woman's name. "Joilyn… I don't know what happened to her, but up until this meeting, I thought she'd died in a car wreck. So did Rattler."

"You *thought* she died? Does that mean she's not dead?"

"It looks that way. It was why we were called to the meeting. A paramilitary group has been hired to rescue a CIA deep cover operative. When this group found out who they were going after, they did some research to prepare for the job. That's when they found out who she was in relation to Grim Road. Which is Rattler's sister."

When he didn't say anything more, but looked like he wanted to, dread built inside my chest until it felt like a lead weight. "What else?" My voice was barely above a whisper.

"Yeah. What else." Falcon looked like he was in so much pain. When he spoke, it was a hoarse rasp, like he was choking on the emotion clearly visible in his expression. And I knew.

"Joilyn. You love her."

"I used to. I'm not ever going to lie to you, Gina. No matter how much it hurts me." He shook his head. "I was supposed to marry her. She died. That was more than two years ago. I might not have known she was alive, but she knew how to contact me, and she never did. So it doesn't matter if I still love her or not."

"Yes, it does, Falcon. Your feelings matter." I ducked my head and he let me, resting his hands on my knees as he stayed on his knees. "I understand this must be a shock to you."

"Yeah. It is. I'm still processing, but Joilyn isn't the important thing right now."

"You said these people were supposed to rescue her. You're going with them. That's why you have to leave. Isn't it?"

"It is. They've given me and Rattler the opportunity to go with them. Even if I'm not with Joilyn anymore, I can't leave her safety in the hands of someone else. Not even men I know are competent. She's Rattler's sister. The three of us grew up together and relied on each other until we were adults. Even then, we had each other's backs. No matter what. Rattler and I went into the Marines right after high school, and we sent money home to Joilyn so she could go to college. She was the smart one. Me and Rattler were grunts."

"Sounds like you admired her a lot."

"I did."

"What do you think happened? I mean, with the car accident and where she's been all this time."

"That's something I want to find out, but it's not the reason I have to go with the team assigned to rescue her."

"I don't understand." I was so fucking close to tears, I knew there would be no way to get much farther before I broke down. Christ, this was going to hurt. Because I could already tell there was no way I could measure up to this woman.

"Me and Rattler hadn't been here long. We were still prospects when Rocket and Lemon first got together. Before that, we'd just come off a mission where my whole fuckin' team was killed. Eight men and women. Rattler and me were the only two who made it. Today we learned there was a third person on that mission."

"Joilyn?" My heart pounded. It was one more way this woman was better than me. If she'd been on the same mission Falcon had been on, did that mean she was a soldier too? Had she sacrificed her safety and freedom in the name of service? Even knowing I was likely to lose Falcon to this woman, I couldn't hate her.

"Yeah, baby. She was the agency's asset on the inside of that terror cell. No one told me and Rattler or we'd have burned down the fuckin' earth to bring her home. And she's been there ever since. Two fuckin' years. The one thing I always promised anyone under my command was something I heard in a movie once. As a warrior, it made sense to me. Dead or alive, we all come home together. I've never left anyone. The fact it was Joilyn makes it so much worse."

"Because she was your fiancée."

"Because she was someone I considered family."

"I understand. You need to bring her home."

"I do, baby."

I gave him a tremulous smile as tears overflowed and spilled down my cheeks. Falcon stood and pulled me to my feet. Instead of stepping back, though, he lifted me into his arms and picked me up. He carried me to the couch, then sat, positioning me so I straddled him and rested his hands on my hips. His expression seemed more relaxed. He wasn't at ease by any means, but I thought maybe what he'd told me about him and Rattler and Joilyn had been something he needed off his chest.

More, I now knew he blamed himself for the death of his team. He hadn't come out and said it that way, but for whatever reason, he felt like he'd failed them in some very important way. "I promise you, Gina, I will come back. I'll get Joilyn back to safety, then I'm coming home." He met my gaze and held it steadily. "To you. Then we'll have a long talk about what we both want."

"Just promise you'll let me know you're safe. When you get back. You don't have to see me again if you don't want to." It hurt. God, it hurt! Falcon was a protector first and foremost. Sure, he tried to hide it under a macho exterior, but I could see that side of him in the way he'd taken care of me these last few months. There was no way he could turn his back on a woman he loved. And that woman wasn't me. It was the woman he was supposed to marry.

"Listen to me, Gina. Really listen." When I gave him a shaky nod, he continued. "I'm. Comin'. Back. For. *You*." He said each word slowly and distinctly. "I can't trust anyone but Rattler to get Joilyn out of whatever hellhole she's in. But once she's safe, I'm comin' home. *To you*. Do you understand me?"

"I -- I don't -- I don't know." I sobbed out the response, the dam holding back my emotions beginning to fail.

"I know I haven't exactly earned your trust yet, but I'm asking for it. Just this once. Give me the chance to prove myself to you."

I slowly lowered my forehead to his and sighed. The tears came faster -- it was becoming impossible to hold them back. I wanted this with everything in my being. I wanted Falcon. But I was desperately afraid my reality didn't account for a man like Falcon. He deserved a whole woman. I was fragmented into so many pieces, there was no way to put me back together without some lingering cracks.

"God, Falcon." I took in another shuddering breath. "Please, I'm begging you, don't break my heart any more than it's already breaking."

He wrapped his arms around me then, squeezing me to him tightly. "Never, baby. I'm not ever gonna try to sell you somethin' I don't fully mean. I will come back. I will come to you. I'll make sure you are given updates as often as possible and I will call you the first chance I'm able when we're out safely."

"You promise this isn't a line of bullshit? Because I'm not sure I could handle it if you're not sincere."

"I'm completely sincere." He rubbed my back up and down in a soothing caress. "Like I said. I will never lie to you. I'm done denying I want you for my own, Gina. Because, the more I get to know you, the more I love just being with you. So, I'm gonna do what I have to because, no matter what led her to this point in her life, Joilyn is still my best friend's sister. She made her choice. Now, I've made mine."

Falcon turned my face up to his and took my lips in a tender, soul-destroying kiss. His lips were a silky glide over mine, his tongue lapping softly. He coaxed me to open for him and, when I did, he slid inside my mouth briefly. He teased me, but I didn't feel overwhelmed or pressured. It felt like a promise. A promise of what he could do to me if I let him. Of how good he could make sex between us. I already knew the latter. I knew part of the former, but I had the feeling we'd only scratched the surface of what he could make my body give him. I might not have been willing in the strictest sense of the word, but I couldn't deny Falcon had pleasured me as much as I had him. Nothing he'd done to me had felt like an assault then, and I didn't think about our encounters as anything other than pleasurable now. If my feelings weren't normal, I guess I just wasn't normal.

Falcon pulled back to look into my eyes. I felt like I was drowning. In him. "Falcon..."

"I'm right here, baby. Not goin' anywhere right now. I'm stayin' with you as long as I can before we pull out."

"I need..." I swallowed. "I need to tell you something."

His eyes narrowed. "You can tell me anything."

"You never... hurt me. Not once. I was ashamed to admit it at the time, but I liked what we did together."

Instantly, Falcon stiffened. I knew this was a bad idea, but I needed him to know this. "I'm so fuckin' sorry, Gina. If I'd thought for one second that fuckin' bastard Hammer was lyin' to us when he said you were OK with him sharin' you, I'd never have... I'd never..."

"I know. You're a good man, Falcon. I see it every single day."

"I'd have gotten you away from Hammer, Gina." There was so much emotion in his voice. He swallowed several times as if he were choking on all those feelings bottled up inside him. "I'd have protected you."

I smiled at him. "I believe that more than anything. You're a protector. I don't blame you for what happened. I couldn't when I got as much enjoyment as I did. Not only that, but you were always kind." I smiled, ducking my head again as I picked at the collar of his T-shirt. "I thought of you as the gentleman biker. You looked so rough around the edges and all dangerous with your tattoos and scars, but you were unfailingly kind to me. And you always, always asked me if I was still good with the situation. You didn't press, but you asked. To me, that meant more than anything. The way I see it, it was my fault for lying to you."

"No. None of that was your fault. None of it."

"No. I know it wasn't. But it wasn't yours either."

He smiled. "You're a remarkable woman, Gina. I'll be proud to have you on the back of my bike."

For some reason, I felt a smile tug at my lips. Maybe I was deluding myself. Maybe he'd change his mind when he got Joilyn back -- and I knew he'd get her back. Falcon didn't have "quit" in him when it came to something like this. So, maybe he would decide to go back to her. Until he did, though, I was going to pretend he meant what he'd just said. I'd worry about the aftermath later. For now, I was going to enjoy being with the only man I'd ever be able to love in any kind of meaningful way. I was going to take whatever he chose to give me and live in the moment. Tomorrow would work itself out. I'd deal with whatever happened when it happened because I refused to waste energy on borrowed trouble. Life was too fucking short.

Chapter Five

Falcon

I felt like the next two days were leading up to my execution. I knew whatever happened in the following days would change my life forever but I wasn't sure which way it was going to go. So I refused to think about it. Instead, I spent every waking moment either pestering Scout, the ExFil team leader who'd contacted me and Rattler, or with Gina.

Right now, Gina and I were in her backyard. We lay on fucking pool lounge chairs. The sun filtered through the trees providing the perfect amount of light and warmth. I'd grilled hotdogs because I couldn't cook anything but omelets for shit, and opened a can of pork and beans for lunch. It was the first time we'd done anything like this, and I was already mentally kicking my own ass for not coaxing her out sooner.

Gina had a genuine smile on her face as she ate nearly burnt hotdogs and sopped up the bean juice with her hotdog bun. She chatted lightly about any topic I distracted her with. I did not mention my imminent departure. Or Joilyn.

"If I'd known you were this great at grilling hotdogs, I'd have invited you over for this sooner." She gave me a bright smile. It struck me that this was the happiest I'd seen her since I'd met her. Even before we all found out the hell Hammer had put her through, her act had fooled us all. Including me. I also hadn't realized how different her fake smiles were from her genuine ones.

Daylight and dark.

I snorted into my beer bottle. "They're burnt, baby."

She gave me a big smile. "Exactly! Soooo good!"

She took a bite and actually rolled her eyes in what looked like ecstasy. Which… yeah. All my brain cells went straight to my cock and I absolutely would not acknowledge my fucking hardon.

We finished, and I disposed of the paper plates. When I came back, she'd scooted her chair closer to mine so we were close enough to touch. After I sat down, she tentatively reached over and took my hand in hers. Her palms were slightly sweaty and her hands trembled. I could see the pulse pounding in her neck.

She didn't look at me, but kept her gaze ahead as if she were studying something beyond the yard. I smiled softly at her, even though she wasn't looking. I turned my hand so our fingers laced together, and Gina instantly relaxed and she let out a breath she'd been holding. Gina clung to me, her grip tightening almost reflexively.

"It's going to be all right, Gina." I spoke softly, not wanting to upset her.

"Sure," she agreed with a smile. But it was one of her fake smiles. I knew them well because it was those smiles she'd used to greet me with.

With a heavy sigh, I tugged her until I could urge her to crawl onto my lounge chair and into my lap. I wrapped my arms around her and cuddled her close. It took her a few seconds, but she finally relaxed and snuggled against me.

Under the canopy of leaves, with the soft rustle of the wind as our only music, we sat in silence. It was a comfortable quiet, a shared respite. I knew Gina needed this moment of peace as much as I did, maybe even more. She'd been through so much, her resilience constantly tested by the storms of her past.

The sun began its descent, painting the sky in shades of orange and pink. It was beautiful, almost painfully so, reflecting how fleeting moments like this could be. I tightened my hold on Gina slightly, not enough to constrict but enough for her to feel my strength surrounding her. At least, I hoped that's how she felt. Because I'd do anything to protect her. I hated to leave her, but I couldn't turn my back on Rattler or Joilyn.

"When do you leave?" Her voice was soft. I loved the feel of her lips against my skin where she burrowed against my shoulder. If I had my way, we'd stay like this forever.

"First light." I knew I needed to reassure her. I just wasn't sure what to say.

She exhaled slowly, her breath stirring the fine hairs on my neck. It was a warm, intimate moment -- the kind that branded itself on your heart and soul, impossible to forget or ignore.

"Thank you," she murmured, her voice muffled against my throat. "For this... for today."

I kissed the top of her head, breathing in the scent of her shampoo, a mix of vanilla and something floral. "You're welcome," I whispered back. "Anything for you, baby. Anything." I meant every word. She brought out a fierce protectiveness in me that I'd tried so hard to bury deep. For my own sanity. But it was really impossible. I felt the same need to find Joilyn and get her to safety. But it was somehow different. Probably the time that had passed, combined with my sense of betrayal that Joilyn had been alive all along and hadn't bothered to contact me or Rattler to let us know what was going on.

I could feel the tension slowly ebb from her body. I stroked her hair gently, feeling the soft strands slip between my fingers. The sun dipped lower, stretching our shadows across the lawn like long, dark ribbons until darkness enveloped us in a warm breeze. The tops of the trees were silhouetted against the remaining light in the sky.

"You probably need to get some sleep," she murmured.

"I'm perfectly fine right where we are." I wanted to puff out my chest when she nuzzled my shoulder and neck with a contented sigh.

"Me too."

At some point we dozed off. I woke knowing we weren't alone. A moment later, Lemon sat in the chair Gina had vacated for my lap.

"Did you tell her?" Lemon spoke softly, obviously not wanting to wake Gina.

"Yeah. I told her everything I know to this point, including about my relationship with Joilyn."

"Good. I don't have to tell you to make sure you know what you're doing before you leave here. Right?"

"Lemon, now ain't the time."

She gave me a hard look and I had the immediate urge to give in to whatever demands she made. Somehow, though, I managed to quash the impulse. "She deserves to know what to expect when you come back, Falcon. She's a good person. None of this should have ever happened to her."

"You think I don't know that?" The question came out harsher than I intended, and Gina whimpered in her sleep, shifting slightly and clinging tighter to my shirt with one small fist. "She's the sweetest person in the world. She loves the kids in the compound and is always making them cookies or some other sickly-sweet treat they absolutely love. I've wanted nothing other than to make her my old lady since the day I fuckin' met her, but I couldn't." My chest tightened with emotion as I remembered those days. "Then Crush warned us to back off but wouldn't say why."

"Everyone said they stopped coming to her after Crush and Byte spread the word. Did you?" She raised one blonde eyebrow. "I mean, really?"

"Yeah, Lemon. At least I never went to her for sex again. But I did make a point to talk to her when I could. To be nice to her. Hell, that fuckin' pink-ass bike I drive now will probably be permanent because I think that's when she decided maybe I was all right."

"No accounting for taste." Lemon was nothing if not blunt and we had a standing feud in which, I'm not too ashamed to admit, she routinely kicked my ass. "But I suppose she could have done worse. Any guy who gives up his man card to ride a pink bike so he can bring some joy to a traumatized woman is OK in my book."

I blinked, my eyes widening. This wasn't like the vice president at all. She was the woman who still called me Pigeon Nuts because of our first encounter. Rocket had been in trouble and I'd refused to put the club at risk. It was standard operating procedures at the time. She'd been furious with me. "Christ, Lemon. Are you... are you fuckin' dyin' or somethin'? Because if you are, you don't have to say anything positive about me. I give you permission to call me Pigeon Nuts." I winced even as I said it.

Lemon let out a bark of laughter, and Gina started awake. "Wassat?"

"Hush, honey." I stroked her hair. "Everythin's fine. Lemon dropped by."

Gina sat up and tried to stand, but I stayed her with my hands firmly on her hips. She gave me a nervous look before giving Lemon one of her fake smiles. "Hi, Lemon. I'm glad you stopped by." I could tell she was anything but glad, but decided not to say anything. Mostly because I thought I knew why she was wary.

Lemon snorted but grinned at Gina, chuckling lightly. "No, you're not. Which is exactly why I turned up." She sat on the edge of the lounge chair sideways, her elbows resting on her knees. Lemon reached over and took one of Gina's hands in both of hers. "This is your home, Gina. No matter what. We're your family."

"I know." Gina smiled, but again, it was her fake smile.

Lemon studied the other woman for several seconds before shaking her head. "I don't think you do. Grim Road has a few other chapters over the country. If things are uncomfortable, the guys can transfer. Rocket says members patch over for different reasons. They'd all still have the club's protection, but you'd be comfortable in your home."

Gina frowned and shook her head. "That doesn't seem fair."

"Honey, what's fair is none of this ever happening to you. I'm glad you landed here. I just wish things had gone down differently."

"I'm glad I'm here too, Lemon. Thank you for everything you've done for me."

Lemon shrugged. "We're sisters. That's what sisters do." Then she gave Gina a wide smile. "Me and the girls are gonna stay with you while the guys are playing in their flying tin cans. We can have a big party with every kind of pizza we can get our hands on. Chips. Beer. Wine. Crown Royal. It'll be awesome!"

Gina let out a small giggle and I saw her genuine smile break through for a moment. Yeah. She liked the idea but was anxious. "Why not just skip the food altogether?"

"See? This is what I'm talkin' about! Woman after my own heart." Lemon raised a hand for a high five and Gina complied with a grin and she started to relax again.

"We should probably get some rest, Lemon." I couldn't fuck Gina before I left, but there was no way in hell I was gonna spend my last night before this mission anywhere other than wrapped around her as she slept.

"Yeah. I'll come with Rocket when he and Knox pick up Falcon and Rattler. You can go back to bed if you want and I'll be here if you need me."

"Lemon, why have you always been so nice to me? Is it because you feel sorry for me?"

Lemon held Gina's gaze for several moments before she answered her. "Gina, you are one of the strongest women I know. You walked through fire and made it out the other side alive. Singed, but alive. Not only that, you're taking your life back. You're learning to trust again. It takes a brave person to take the leap. So you'll always have my respect."

This was one of many reasons Lemon was vice president of Grim Road. She always seemed to know the exact right -- or wrong -- thing to say or do. It was her superpower. She squeezed Gina's hands before standing to leave.

Gina didn't move other than to bunch her hand back into my shirt. "I don't want you to go." Her soft whisper wrapped around my heart and squeezed. "It's selfish, I know. And I don't expect you to really not go, but I still don't want you to."

"Honey, if it was anyone other than Joilyn, I'd gladly tell everyone to piss off. But I can't."

"I know. It's who you are."

"Come on. How about we go inside and watch a movie before bed?"

She settled back against me, clutching my shirt once more. "Maybe we could stay here a little while longer?"

I kissed the top of her head again. "Of course, baby. As long as you like."

* * *

Gina

If it gave me a little bit of a reprieve having to think about him leaving me to go rescue the woman who he'd planned on marrying, then I'd take it. I believed Falcon when he said he'd come back, but I wasn't all certain he'd want to stay with someone like me when he had a second chance at a happy ever after.

Chapter Six

Falcon

Once Gina was asleep, I carefully stood and carried her to bed. She never let go of my shirt. Even in her sleep. She was breaking my fucking heart!

I lay with her cuddled against my chest for most of the remaining hours before I had to leave. It was about an hour before I needed to get up when Gina stirred against me.

"What time is it?" Her words were slurred slightly from sleep.

"Three-thirty."

"What time do you have to leave?"

"Five."

She raised herself slightly so she looked down at me. Moonlight spilled through the bedroom window to bathe her face in a silvery glow. She looked ethereal, almost unreal. She lay her palm against my beard-roughened cheek. Then she kissed me. It was a light pressing of lips but she lingered.

God, I'd missed her kisses. She was sweetly tentative and her lips trembled slightly against mine.

"Baby," I whispered to her between kisses.

"I want you, Falcon." Her voice wavered, and I thought I tasted tears on her lips. "Please."

"I'll pleasure you, baby, but I'm not takin' you. Not until this is over. It wouldn't be right."

"Even if I asked you to?"

"Especially if you asked me to. Honey, when you come to me, when you tell me you're ready for me to fuck you, it's not gonna be right before I leave. And it's especially not gonna be when you're worried about what's gonna happen when I get home." Very slowly, I rolled us over and settled my weight between her legs.

She eagerly wrapped hers around my waist, tempting me with what we both wanted. "When I take you, it's gonna be with the full knowledge that I'm never letting you go, Gina. You can't believe me when I tell you I'll be back for you. I understand, and that's OK."

"I never realized how chatty you were," she grumbled before pulling me down for another kiss.

I had to chuckle against her lips. I wanted her more than I'd ever wanted a woman in my life! That I couldn't have her was a gnawing pain, but it was more emotional than physical. She was one more person in my life I cared for that I could let down. She was strong, but so very fragile in many ways.

"Yeah, I'm a real chatterbox." I kissed her neck before pushing off of her. "Do you want me to make you come, Gina?"

She sucked in a breath. "You'll fuck me?"

I gave her a wry grin. "Afraid not. But I'll eat your pussy until you scream. If that's what you want."

Looking away from me, Gina bit her bottom lip. I was afraid I might have pushed her too far, then she raised her arms to me and wound them around my neck. "I think I want that more than just about anything right now."

Her words sent a shiver of anticipation down my spine. "Take off your shirt and shorts for me, baby. Your underwear too. Let me see your beautiful body."

As she wiggled out of her clothes, I took the moment to whip off my shirt. I couldn't fuck her, but I could press her naked body to mine. I needed the skin to skin contact with her. Even if it was only for a short time.

Once she was naked, I lowered myself to her, feeling the heat of her body rise to meet mine. The room was silent except for the soft rustle of the sheets and our mingled breaths. Carefully, I kissed her again, deeply, drinking in the moment, knowing it might need to last me through the coming days.

"Hold onto me," I murmured against her lips, and she did, her fingers threading through my hair, pulling me closer.

I trailed kisses down her neck, each one a promise, a memory I wanted her to cling to while I was gone. By the time I reached her breasts, she was breathing heavily, her body arching toward me as if pulled by some magnetic force. My hands roamed over her skin, memorizing every curve and dip as though they were topography I needed to navigate by heart.

When my mouth finally found its way between her legs, Gina gasped sharply. Her grip on my hair tightened and her hips canted to my mouth.

"Mmm…" I hummed against her pussy, swiping my tongue from pussy to clit.

"Falcon!"

I smiled, feeling a mix of triumph and tenderness as I kissed her pussy once more. "That's my girl," I murmured. The mood shifted from heavy emotion to a gentler, more intimate connection as I prepared to make good on my promise of making her come.

Gina's breath hitched in anticipation as she watched me, her eyes dark with desire and something more -- maybe hope, maybe fear. I could taste the urgency of this moment, knowing it was critical not only for the pleasure it promised but also for the reassurance I hoped to give her.

Every touch was calculated to comfort and excite as I traced my fingers along her inner thighs, eliciting shivers and soft moans that fueled my own desires. But tonight, it wasn't about my needs. It was all for Gina, to give her something pure and unrestrained.

As I focused on her, everything else faded away -- the looming mission, the uncertainty of what lay ahead -- all of it dissolved into the background. All that mattered was Gina and the connection that pulsed between us, electric and undeniable.

I intensified my attention, circling and flicking her clit with precision, guided by her sharp intakes of breath and the way her body moved against me. Her hands in my hair grew more insistent, urging me closer. She was about to come. I could feel the tension coiling tightly within her.

"Gina," I whispered against her skin, my voice rough with desire and an aching tenderness. "Let go for me, baby."

Her response was a strangled cry, her body arching as she reached that crest. She screamed, a sound that echoed off the walls and reverberated deep in my chest. Her climax washed over her in waves, and I held her through it all, my mouth still working gently to bring her down as softly as I could.

She cried out again, a sound mingled with my name and something like relief. In the aftermath, she lay trembling, her breaths coming in jagged sighs.

I pressed a gentle kiss to her bare mound before I crawled up beside her, our sweaty torsos sticking slightly as I pulled her into my arms. She nestled against my chest, still catching her breath. Her fingers traced idle patterns on my skin as we both lay there in the quiet.

"I'm scared," she whispered after a while. Her voice was so faint I might have missed it if not for the stillness of the room. "I don't want to lose you."

"I know you're scared. You're not gonna lose me, honey. Not as long as you'll have me." My hand stroked her hair in long, slow strokes. It soothed me.

Like petting a contented kitten. "I swear it."

"You don't know that. What if she has a perfectly reasonable explanation and wants you back? What if she needs you?"

"Like I said, baby. She had any number of opportunities to let me know she was alive if she'd wanted to. Before she went over there to infiltrate that cell, anyway."

"Sounds like she's a hero." Gina didn't sound wistful or anything, just resigned.

"Yeah. If what Rocket was told is true, then yes. She is."

"You know, I can never be that kind of woman. I'm not built for it."

"Did anyone say you had to be a covert operative to be a hero? Sunshine and Rainbow think you're a hero. Effie and Aneshya think you're a hero. Luke too."

"I don't know about that. They like my cookies."

"You think that's why all of them, even Luke, are at your house several times a week begging for cooking lessons? Aneshya swears she's gonna be a chef. Effie says she's going to open her own bakery when she grows up. And Lemon caught Luke building a Cookies and Lemonade stand for the girls. You don't think they'd have been so excited about all that if you hadn't come into their lives, do you?"

She shrugged. "They might have."

I chuckled and pulled her closer. "No, baby. They wouldn't. Now. I need to get ready. I'll come say goodbye before I leave. Let Lemon look after you. She'll never admit it, but I think she needs to mother everyone. You'll be doing me a favor because if she's fussing over you, I might get started on this mission without her calling me Pigeon Nuts in front of anyone." As I'd hoped, that got a small laugh from her.

"That wasn't much, but I'll take it." I smiled before kissing her once more, then heading to the bathroom to get ready.

Thirty minutes later, dressed and my duffle packed, I sat on the edge of the bed and once again, stroking my hand down the length of Gina's hair. She blinked up at me, tears glistening in her lovely, copper-colored eyes.

"Be safe while I'm gone."

"You're the one going into danger. You be safe. I'll be fine in the compound."

"I'm telling Rocket and Lemon you're my old lady. The club would look after you anyway, but if something happens to me, I want it official so there's no pushback." Then I frowned. "Except Lemon won't allow there to be pushback. But I still want you to have my protection. So, while I'm gone, I'll have Lemon put in an order for your property cut."

Gina didn't really look convinced, but I could see how badly she wanted this. Wanted to be mine. I knew she was nervous. Under normal circumstances I'd never leave her for something like this. Especially not when our relationship was this new. But I couldn't let this go. I might not have known Joilyn was part of my team, but she still was. Which, in my mind, made it my responsibility to get her back. And I would. I was done letting down people I cared about.

"I'll look forward to it," she said softly, giving me a sad smile.

"Good. Get some rest. I'll be back before you know it."

Chapter Seven

Gina

I spent most of my time at home. In my house. Lemon and some of the girls had come by every day, but I just couldn't get out and walk around the compound. It had only been twenty-four hours since Falcon left, but I had fallen into despondency. The man I was in love with was on a mission to save the woman he was supposed to marry. No reason to be down about that, right? Yeah, I was moping and I knew it.

I was curled up on the couch when I heard feminine laughter outside my door right before there was a loud pounding as someone knocked heavily.

"Open up, Gina! It's time for you to party. With us." Was that Lemon?

I stood and walked to the door. I was in leggings and the shirt Falcon had left in my bedroom. Silly, but it made me feel closer to him when I was fairly certain everything would change when he came back. When I opened the door, all the old ladies in Grim Road were there.

"Hi, Gina!" Olivia was the sweetest person. Her man, Bear, was one of the biggest men I'd ever seen. Appropriate as far as I was concerned. "We brought snacks and alcohol. We're gonna watch the *Great British Baking Show* and get schnozzled!" She gave me a bright smile along with a tight hug. "Everything's gonna be fine. Lemon won't let it be any other way."

Cecilia was next in hugging me. Of all the old ladies, Cecilia was the one I gravitated to the most. She'd been forced into prostitution. Bullet had claimed her after she'd been beaten nearly to death. We weren't close, but I thought she might be the one woman in the club I semi-related to. And only because of what I'd gone through from Hammer in this same club.

"Lemon raided Bullet's stash of fruit punch. My advice is to lay off anything else if you drink any." Cecilia grinned. "Small sips over at least an hour."

Evelyn and Calista were next, each woman greeting me warmly. All the old ladies at Grim were wonderful. They'd all helped me so much. Lemon and her sister, Apple, had helped first. Lemon had been the one to get my story out of me. Then she had started the process of getting rid of my nightmare. As each woman had been claimed by one of Grim Road's members, they'd all been around regularly. If Lemon or their men had told them what had happened to me, none of them ever said. They never failed to check on me or include me in any family events held in this area of the compound.

"The kids wanted to come too," Lemon said, "but sometimes bitches need some bitch time with other bitches." That got a laugh from everyone. Even me.

We all piled into the living room, settling on my mismatched assortment of couches and chairs. Olivia popped open a bag of popcorn while Cecilia began setting up the TV for our baking show marathon. Calista brought in covered trays of snacks. There were cookies, chips, and even some homemade dips. Evelyn found a comfy corner on the sofa with a sizeable glass of punch she balanced on a small table beside her. I assumed this was the punch Cecilia had been talking about, but figured I'd ask before consuming any. I wasn't averse to getting stoned, I just didn't want any surprises.

This was the first time I'd really appreciated the friendship and solidarity these women always projected with each other. Even though I rarely let myself be drawn into their circle, this time, there was no doubt I was part of this exclusive sorority. These women were here because I needed them. Lemon had likely put out the call and they'd all answered.

Lemon sat down next to me, handing me a glass filled with ice and Bullet's notorious fruit punch, along with a big dollop of ice cream. Her eyes met mine, fierce yet kind. "We've got your front, side, and back, Gina. We always have. We always will." It was a soft exchange just between the two of us and I found myself smiling. Lemon gripped my shoulder before sitting back and propping her feet on the coffee table next to mine. "Stop thinking about what might happen when Falcon returns. Focus on now. We're all here and we care about you. Besides, if Falcon doesn't realize what a perfect old lady he would have with you, he really does have pigeon nuts."

I couldn't help but smile. I'd heard Lemon call Falcon Pigeon Nuts more than once. It always made Falcon scowl, but I thought he didn't mind it as much as he let on. I got the feeling that was just the way he and Lemon got along.

"You're right. I really appreciate all you guys have done for me. Both now and since all that shit… you know. Before." She was right, but I found it hard to shake off the heaviness in my chest. Lemon was good at many things, including reading people. She knew just how to coax someone out of their shell or, when needed, to give them a shove. The latter was never subtle.

It didn't take long for everyone to have a running, laughing commentary on each challenge in the show. Between bouts of laughter and sips of punch, I began to feel lighter, almost buoyant. Despite my initial reluctance, being surrounded by these wonderful women was slowly peeling away layers of my anxiety. Evelyn passed around a plate of cookies she'd baked herself, insisting they were better than anything on the baking show. "You see, it's all about adding that extra bit of love," she said, and winked.

"Christ, Evie." Apple rolled her eyes. "Can you get any more cheesy?"

We all laughed and Evelyn threw a pillow at Apple, hitting her in the face. Apple laughed until tears rolled down her cheeks, as did Evelyn.

The rest of the night was spent binge watching the rest of the current season. By the time the winner was decided, we were all drooping. And I was more than a little whacked from the fruit punch. Me and Lemon managed to get some blankets and pillows for everyone and we piled up on couch and chair cushions in the middle of the floor like kids at a sleepover.

I suppose that's what it was. I'd never had one, but it seemed fitting that these women were the ones at my first sleepover.

As I lay next to Cecilia, I looked at the other woman. She was on her side facing me and reached out her hand to grasp mine tightly. "It's going to be all right, Gina. Lemon won't let it be anything else."

"Yeah. I should have realized that. Sooner." The woman was a force of nature.

"Falcon and Lemon are at each other's throats most days, but she respects him. He'd have to be a good man to earn Lemon's respect."

"I know he's a good man. I don't know many men who would ride around on a pink bike just because I enjoy it."

Cecilia grinned and squeezed my hand again. "See? That's true love right there."

We both laughed, but I was ashamed to admit

how that simple observation helped me relax. It was either that or the pot in the fruit punch. Could be either, but I thought it was that damned pink bike.

I closed my eyes and drifted for a long time before I finally let sleep drag me under. Then I didn't move until morning.

Chapter Eight

Falcon

"Hard to believe the one place that gives me fuckin' nightmares is in fuckin' Oklahoma." Rattler muttered his objection as we approached the big ranch house where we thought Joilyn was being held. Crush and Byte had hooked up with ExFil's intelligence crew and were helping coordinate the rescue. It wasn't something Cain would normally allow, but the man understood our situation. Besides that, I thought he was trying to recruit some of Grim Road's members to ExFil.

"We still looking at thirteen people on the grounds?" I peered through my field glasses, trying to spot as many people as I could. The last thing I wanted was to accidentally cut through the path of one guard trying to avoid another.

"Yep. Thirteen plus your girl," Scout answered from my earpiece. He and another ExFil agent were on one side of the structure while me and Rattler were with three other ExFil team members.

"These guys look like they know what they're doing." I thought that was a guy called Goose. He and the team sniper, Deadeye, were positioned on a small hill about three hundred yards away. About the time he commented, someone ran out of the house, stumbling down the stairs, and bent over as he braced himself on the porch. Looked like he was puking. "At least, some of them know what they're doing." The last was a dry mutter.

"Data says he's only found one device on any network in the house or surrounding areas," Scout muttered. If he was anything like the rest of the team, he had his eyes firmly on the target.

Of our group, two out of the three were studying the house with binoculars. The third guy constantly swept the surrounding area but without the field glasses. His name was Chase. I thought he'd been part of a shady organization before he'd ended up in Bones MC with Cain and most of the ExFil team here currently.

"*One*?" I couldn't help the question. "You mean like they truly are off the grid?"

"Seems that way. Cheetah, what are you seeing?" Cheetah was in her forties and one of the most cheerful people I'd ever met. It was almost sickening but the damned woman had me in stitches before we'd left for this operation, laughing at wartime stories of this team and others she'd served with. Goose had told me she had a knack for picking up on people's emotions and had known I was tense. I liked her immediately. She was completely different once we stepped in the vehicle to start this.

"Female target is in an upstairs room on the south side. I have a partial visual on her and it looks like she's shackled. I don't see her being out of line of sight without someone freeing her first."

"Good, Cheetah. You're in charge of her." Scout gave orders like a man well used to this kind of operation. He was thoughtful and deliberate, but confident in every intel question and every command given. "Deke, you have Cheetah's back."

"Roger."

"Deadeye, follow Cheetah, Deke, and Joilyn when they get her out of the house. Don't fire unless our team does first. That fifty cal is loud enough to wake half the fuckin' state."

"No promises, Scout." Though his words

sounded defiant, it was Deadeye's version of humor. I'd learned that in the first few hours after meeting the team. They said the man lightened up a little after meeting his woman, but if this was lighter, I'd have hated to see him before he'd met her.

"Tool. Clutch. Take our guests and go hunting." Scout's command was hard as steel. Unbending. "No one leaves this place alive except us and Joilyn." That was our cue to get this fuckin' shit over with.

The four of us took off toward the ranch, crouching in the tall brush grass. The moon was bright and only half obscured through the clouds but still brighter than I'd like. I was glad for the night vision goggles we'd been issued, even if the things were clunky as shit. Laughter filtered to us as the guys in front made fun of their buddy currently bent double and vomiting everything he'd ever eaten since conception. Much as I hated giving these guys a reprieve, the noise was the cover we needed if Scout was intent on making as little noise as possible.

"Leave the dumbasses up front?" I whispered, already starting to make my way around them before Scout confirmed my request.

"The guys on the perimeter got little to no LOS on the guys in the back. Falcon, go with Tool and take the eastern perimeter. Rattler and Clutch can take the west. Cheetah, once those two teams meet in the back to take out the rest outside the house, you and Deke start your move inside the house. Should be good to move once you get there. Sound off as each area is clear."

Yeah. If only things always went that smooth. The closer we moved to the house, the more my anxiety ratcheted up. If there was any doubt this place had given me PTSD, it was erased. I kept expecting to hear shots ringing out, people screaming. As I looked to my left, I spotted Rattler and fully expected to see his head explode. It had happened the last time. I'd turned to give an order and the man to my left had been shot with a gun so big, his head disintegrated.

I tried to shake it off and keep moving forward. It was hard, though. The kills were easy. It was the one thing I could do to keep the panic at bay. We had to go slow, so I could concentrate on each movement and keep myself aware of where the rest of my team was.

Once we made it behind the house, I had firm control of my emotions. Yes, I was still stressed. I doubted I'd be able to relax until I was back in the Grim Road compound. And I wasn't altogether certain it was because I felt safe there.

Everyone sounded off their kill as we cleared the perimeter around the house.

My gaze found Rattler's when we raised our night vision as we entered the house ahead of Cheetah and Deke. He gave a short nod and we started a search of the house.

"Front room, east side," Goose said over the radio. "Spotted two guys in front of the window."

"I got 'em," someone acknowledged.

"Whoever has the phone just made a call." I didn't recognize this man's voice either, but suspected it was one of the computer guys with ExFil.

"I got him." Crush's voice was immediate. Just knowing one of my own men was listening in, helping, eased my anxiety drastically. "Going to a local number three klicks to the north of you. It's a hardware store in town."

"Yeah. These guys own a business. Fine upstanding citizens with a federal agent held hostage in their farmhouse."

That gave me pause. Once we'd cleared the house, I spoke my concerns. "I'm assuming there's a reason local law enforcement -- or any law enforcement, really -- isn't involved with this, Scout?"

"Might shoulda asked that question before you came along, but yeah. There is."

"That'll do, I guess."

"Good. Cheetah. I assume you have the woman?"

"I do. She's a little banged up but not hurt."

That eased my worry for Joilyn, but also sent my mind whirling. "She's been with these fucks for two years. How's she not hurt?"

"Can we save twenty questions for after we're on the road or, preferably, in the air?" Scout was losing his patience.

I ground my teeth together. "Fuckin' hate spooks."

"Same. You know, even though we were employed by them at one time." Rattler moved past me to cover Cheetah when she came downstairs with Joilyn. Deke had the rear so I covered the flank.

The second we stepped into the clearing around Scout and Tool we loaded everything into two trucks. I was with Rattler guarding the trucks in case we missed someone or reinforcements arrived. The last thing we wanted to happen was to get someone hurt now. Scout tapped me on the shoulder and I nudged Rattler. I jumped into the back of one truck, Rattler got in the back of the other, and we all sped off.

The ride to the private airfield where we'd left the plane took an hour, and by the time we pulled into the barn at the front of the strip, I had a raging headache, likely from a combination of adrenaline letdown and trying to focus intently on everything around us. And I had barely laid eyes on Joilyn.

I met Rattler as the team covered Cheetah, Joilyn, and Deke, making them board the plane first. When we were all inside and the plane was in the air bound for Florida, I finally relaxed. I needed a moment to close my eyes and center myself. I'd been so focused on getting everyone in and out without anyone getting killed, I hadn't thought about Joilyn beyond explaining to Gina who she was. Now, I had questions. *A lot* of fucking questions.

Rattler was already in the back of the plane where Joilyn sat with a blanket wrapped around her shoulders while an older woman assessed her injuries. The plane wasn't overly fancy to be a corporate aircraft but was comfortable. Kind of like I imagined a private jet owned by a paramilitary corporation might be. It held our team easily enough with enough room for us to stretch our legs without being in each other's way.

I took a breath and stood to go to Rattler where he sat with Joilyn. My gaze locked on hers and she met mine with what I thought was a mixture of defiance and regret in her expression. It was always hard to read Joilyn. She'd always been able to keep her feelings close to the vest. Looked like she hadn't changed much.

"You're not too worse for wear, dear. I think you'll soon have your strength back." The older woman squeezed Joilyn's shoulder as she stood. The woman turned her gaze on me and Rattler, sticking her hand out to my MC brother. "I'm Mama. I serve Bones MC as their doctor. Cain sometimes uses my services with ExFil. He thought Joilyn would be more comfortable with a woman looking after her, but I think she's OK."

"I'm Rattler and this is Falcon." Rattler

introduced us as Mama took my hand in a firm grip. "Joilyn's my sister."

Mama gave me a questioning look.

"I'm Rattler's friend. Joilyn and I had planned on getting married, but that was two years ago." I saw Joilyn's face harden before she masked her expression once more. What the fuck else was I supposed to say? I didn't want to hurt Joilyn, but the fact was, for whatever reason, she'd faked her death long before whatever had happened to put her here.

"I see." Mama gave me a knowing look, like she really did see. She squeezed my arm as she passed me.

I glanced at Rattler who studied his sister intently. The others had given us some privacy by sitting as far forward as they could so we had the back of the plane to ourselves. He crossed the short distance and took Joilyn in a hard embrace and the two clung to each other for long moments. When she pulled back, there was a glimpse of the Joilyn I knew. There was something vulnerable about her before that simply wasn't there now. Rattler was right. I had changed. All three of us had.

"Joi? You're safe now. You know that, right?" Rattler brushed hair off her forehead gently.

Joilyn gave him an angry, impatient look and shoved away from him. "Of course I know I'm safe, Ruben."

Rattler raised an eyebrow. "I only say that because you've been a prisoner for the last two years and all that." There was a bite to his voice I hadn't expected. Probably in response to Joilyn's display of temper. Rattler had never been anything but gentle with his sister. This tone of voice had the tendency to give most men pause.

Joilyn's eyes widened and she actually drew

back slightly before sticking her chin in the air defiantly. "You don't know everything about my life. Everything I did was for a purpose. I stayed embedded in that group as long as I could. It was just my bad luck to have run into someone who knew me in town."

"You mean, someone who thought you were dead?" Yeah, Rattler was good and angry. I couldn't say I blamed him, but given how hard he'd taken her death and how he believed he should have protected Joilyn better, I should have expected him to lash out.

"Easy, Rattler," I murmured. "She's here. She's alive and relatively unharmed. Be thankful you have your sister back."

Rattler closed his eyes, sucking in a breath. Then another one. "You're right. I'm so sorry, Joi." He met his sister's gaze again. "Your death was hard on me." He glanced at me. "On both of us."

"I know. I'm sorry."

I knelt in front of her. "What happened, Joi?" I kept waiting for that sense of betrayal, probably the same thing Rattler was feeling, but it hadn't come. Probably because I was still crashing from the adrenaline letdown.

"Not sure what you mean."

"With you, Joi. Did you fake your own death?"

"Yes." She didn't hesitate. "With the help of the CIA."

"Why?" My question came out more like a demand. Which it was.

She lifted her chin. "That's classified."

"Bullshit." I didn't raise my voice, but didn't let her get away with the cop-out. "You owe me this, Joilyn. You owe both of us an explanation."

"Look. Both of you were already in the Marines. You were serving your country and proud of it. I wanted to do that too."

"No one said you couldn't." Rattler raised his hands in a pleading gesture. "I wouldn't have liked it much, but I'd have helped you all I could. What exactly happened?"

She rubbed her eyes tiredly and winced when a bruise on her face protested. "I did enlist. You guys were deployed. I was going to tell you after basic. But I ticked every box the CIA special ops program was looking for at the time. They said my lack of actual combat experience would work in their favor because they could train me the way they wanted me to operate. The only catch was, I had to leave my life behind. Disappear permanently."

"Christ, Joi! You were eighteen! You couldn't make a decision like that on your own."

"All evidence to the contrary," she replied dryly. Rattler gave her a venomous look and she sighed. "In hindsight, yeah. I can see how it was a bad choice. But I'm not sure discussing it with you would have changed my mind. They were training me to do important things. Things to keep our country safe. I was going to make a difference and I did. The work I did in Oklahoma helped head off at least three different major domestic attacks."

"The CIA doesn't operate inside the US, Joilyn."

"Not usually, no. But there is a domestic division. Project MK-ULTRA and the attempt to suppress the Warren Report are just a couple of examples. Not to mention they had an office under a different name in the World Trade Center on 9/11. Officially, we were operating in Oklahoma because we had tracked a foreign national with ties to multiple terrorist originations."

Rattler snorted. "That the company line?"

"Exactly." Joilyn pointed at her brother, like he'd just proved her point. "It was an excuse. A reason for them to be operating in the area when your team got killed."

"So, if you weren't there to stop a terrorist plot, why were you there? And why did you stay there after everything went to shit?"

"It was a hit. Pure and simple."

"A hit. That the CIA took on personally. Even covering and creating excuses for them being there? That makes no sense at all."

"When have you ever known a government agency to make sense?"

I raised an eyebrow at Rattler. "She's got you there."

"Not helping, Falcon."

"Not trying to. And I'm not buying it."

"It took me a while to figure out what was going on and who I could trust. And I'm talking about people inside the agency. Staying with this bunch was a calculated risk, but I knew I could manage these guys. They're mean, resourceful, and great at hunting squirrels and deer. But well versed in covert ops, they are not. Once I was in with them, I played the part easily enough. Since I didn't have to contact my handler right away because I wasn't sure I could trust him, I didn't risk getting caught. By the time I'd worked it all out, things had died down here and gotten back to normal. Normal being a lesson in paranoid delusions within moderately sized groups. They didn't see women as a threat. Just someone to help them when they needed it. I blended in with the other women, cooking and cleaning and keeping the kids out of the men's way."

"How long had you been in place before the

raid?" Rattler was starting to relax a little. Like me, I was sure he was feeling the adrenaline letdown.

"About six weeks. Not long. Long enough to establish patterns. There wasn't supposed to be anyone but the guys at the house the night of the raid. All of the women and children were supposed to be gone on a picnic off grounds. There weren't that many of us and most of the time, only me and one other woman were there. But that day, it rained. I got word out to my handler, but he said it was too late. The operation had already started.

"I honestly didn't care if the women were there or not. They knew what they were doing, that those guys were homegrown terrorists, and they chose to stay with them. But there was no way I could let those three kids be put in danger. So I sounded the alarm." She closed her eyes and shook her head slightly. One tear slid down her cheek, but she ignored it. "I thought if they were ready, the team coming in would see they'd lost the element of surprise and at least pull back and reassess."

"We questioned that, Rattler," I whispered. "Do you remember?"

"Yeah. We both thought it odd, but I wasn't worried. I knew we could take them."

"We asked for instructions but were told to proceed anyway," Rattler told her. "It wasn't until we saw the kids running toward the property line we realized there were innocents on the ground."

"There were only three kids, but you had no way of knowing there weren't any inside. I knew it would make things difficult, but what I didn't know was how many weapons they had hidden away in the storm cellar, or what kind. I had no fucking idea! I damn sure didn't know about the armor-piercing rounds or the mortars." She shivered. "If I'd been more experienced, or had more time to have studied the place, I'm sure I'd have found their cache. Instead, the timetable got moved up, and there we were."

"You said they were trying to kill someone. Who did they target?"

"Right. One of the guys funding that particular group is the son of an exceedingly wealthy and powerful businessman in the area. He's local, but make no mistake, the man is a silent world powerhouse. As you probably figured out, the place was pretty much completely off the grid. I had to get creative in my digging. Thankfully, I had a few friends in place who I trusted to keep me being alive a secret. We did some work and it looked like the father wanted the son killed. While he is definitely rich enough to kill someone and get away with it, his son being killed might raise a few eyebrows. But, if they could spin it so that it looked like his son had been kidnapped and killed by a bunch of trigger-happy militants bent on blowing up buildings and killing members of law enforcement, he could go on sitting quietly in the shadows. This guy had to have gone to someone high up in the CIA and presented it to set up a smoke screen for future operations inside the US. Kind of like a dress rehearsal in information control in domestic operations."

"Christ, this sounds like something out of a fuckin' movie." Rattler scrubbed a hand over his face in agitation.

"You worked for the fucking CIA too," Joilyn snapped. "Tell me this doesn't sound like something they'd do." When Rattler gave her a look, she continued. "I don't have all the answers, guys. But I do know that the son was trouble. Like the psychotic kind of trouble. And the father'd had all he was gonna take. When the son started plotting to blow up buildings and shoot up parks and courthouses, his father snapped. Rather than have his family name associated with something like the Oklahoma City Bombing, he chose to take the chance it would slip to the press his son was killed in that raid. If the press got wind of his son being killed, the official press release was supposed to play it as his son had been part of a CIA raid. So, of course the press *did* find out. That was the whole point of the mission underneath the mission only a very few people knew about. The report leaked did not say the man was acting with the CIA or against it. Only that he was among the several agents killed during the raid."

My eyes widened. "Felix Newton. He was the son."

"Isn't his dad a US senator or something?" asked Rattler.

Joilyn winced. "Yeah. I'm so going to jail for treason or some shit. 'Cause, you know, that's all classified."

"You're not going to jail," Rattler said firmly. "You'll come back with us. It's why the club exists."

"You mean Grim Road? Yeah, Cheetah said I'd probably be offered the chance to go back with you. She said if I wanted to stay hidden, that's where I needed to go."

"She's right." I thought I should probably reach out to Joilyn, to reassure her she'd have a home with us if she wanted it, but found myself reluctant to take her hand. Instead, I smiled. "The agency knows you're alive because they called ExFil to get you out. Right?"

"That's something that's up for debate." Joilyn eyed me carefully, as if she sensed my reluctance to have physical connection with her. "If my handler didn't tell his superiors, he might have called ExFil himself outside agency channels. It's even possible ExFil thinks they're doing this for the agency when it's really unsanctioned."

"Who's your handler?"

"I only know him by his road name."

"Hello, Joilyn." Scout approached us, reaching out his hand. "I'm Scout."

Her lips parted on a gasp. "Scout? My handler?"

"Yep. That's me. So, to answer your question, no. The CIA doesn't know you're still alive. I'm sorry it took me so long to arrange a rescue."

"Well, it did take me months to contact you. I wasn't sure who I could trust."

"And you waited patiently for me to work with Cain to get things in place to get you outta there. While you did, you were able to get back information that stopped people from being killed. I could have worked something out quicker, but you weren't in immediate danger. I wanted to make sure we did this cleanly. That way you have the option to make a break if you want. We'll help you get a new identity so you can have a normal life."

Joilyn snorted. "Define normal."

"Good point." Scout grinned. "We're headed to Florida. While these guys don't let outsiders in their compound, Salvation's Bane MC's compound will. You can clean up and rest a few days, then decide what you want to do."

Joilyn looked from Rattler to me before nodding her head. "Yeah. That sounds like a good idea."

"And for the record, guys..." Scout raised an eyebrow as his gaze slid from me to Rattler. "She's right about what happened with the raid. The whole thing was an elaborate set-up. What they learned about how information spreads organically before it's picked up by algorithms and shit will be the way they delay information getting to the public in the future."

I stared at Joilyn. Really looked at her. She appeared the same as she did the last day I saw her. Dark auburn hair and green eyes, that stubborn chin and athletic figure were very familiar to me. But I didn't see her the same way I used to. When I thought about marrying a woman, making a home, I didn't see those clear, green eyes looking up at me or the sprinkling of freckles across her nose as she smiled. I saw sparkling copper eyes framed by chestnut-colored ringlets. I saw the look of near hero worship in her eyes when she looked up at me and let my chest swell with pride even though I knew I didn't deserve her. I saw Gina.

I stood to go back to my seat. I had a lot to think about. Mainly about how quickly I could get my property cut around Gina's slim shoulders. The more I thought about it, the more I realized it had been a mistake to come here. Sure, I could say I'd been there for Rattler. The man was my best friend. But the truth was, I'd felt obligated. And maybe a small part of me had thought I wanted her to tell me she hadn't had a choice. I now knew that had been my biggest mistake of all. I didn't want Joilyn. I never had. Not the way I wanted Gina.

"Falcon," Joilyn called out as I walked away. "Can I talk with you before you go up front?" She glanced at Rattler. "Alone?"

"Yeah. Guess we have a lot to talk about."

"Is there someplace private we can go?" Joilyn asked in a louder voice, obviously asking someone else in the plane other than me or Rattler.

Scout looked from me to her and shrugged. "Sure." He led us to a door at the back of the plane. The door opened to a study. There was a small, curved desk in one corner and a leather sectional couch in the other. "It'll be a few hours before we land. Take all the time you need."

He shut the door, and Joilyn and I just stood there. For the first time since I actually got a look at her, she seemed uncertain. Like she was at a loss of how to proceed. Then she crossed the short distance to the couch and sat. I parked my ass on the desk, not knowing exactly what to do. I didn't want to crowd her, and I also needed to keep my distance. The very last thing that could happen now was for her to get the impression I thought we should pick up where we left off.

"You won't sit by me?" She tilted her head looking confused.

"I don't think it's the best idea, Joilyn."

She ducked her head, her hair hiding her face. Then she took a deep breath. "I'm so sorry, Jacob." She'd been so strong and tough up to this point, when her face crumbled and she started weeping silently, it nearly broke my heart. "I thought I was doing the right thing. I wanted to make a difference."

"You did, honey. Scout says you saved lives by staying put."

"I almost got you and Ruben killed," she said softly. "Everyone else died. I know because Scout told me when I first contacted him. That's on me. Isn't it?"

"I don't have answers for questions like that, Joi. But, it honestly doesn't sound like it. You tried to warn us. To keep children from getting caught in the crossfire. I'd rather have died myself than accidentally harmed a child. Besides, their hidden agenda sounded like something they'd say was worth the collateral damage. It's not the people like us in the field who are evil. It's the people pulling our strings to get us to do things we wouldn't normally do. Then, they hold those things over our heads to get us to do more things we wouldn't normally do."

She gave me a startled look, like she was only just now working that out for herself. "So, it wasn't that the operation had already begun. It was that they didn't care."

"I'm afraid so, Joi. Me and Rattler learned those subtleties in the Marines. You went straight into the fire pit. You had no hope of besting anyone in that agency. Manipulation is what they do. The higher in rank, the better they are at it."

"I gave up everything. Didn't I?" She looked devastated and I hurt for her. I really did.

"Not everything. You've still got your brother. And me, but as a friend. As my best friend's sister."

"Like when I was a kid."

"Yeah."

Joilyn looked up at me then, tears swimming in her lustrous eyes. "Did you find someone else?"

I didn't want to hurt her, but there was really no easy way to do this. "I did. It was after I first came to Grim Road. Right after that night."

"So you've been with her for more than a year?"

"No. I met her then, but didn't have a relationship with her until recently."

"So, it's still new?" I wasn't sure I liked the look on Joilyn's face now. It was calculating, where that had never been part of her personality. It set off some alarm bells I wasn't sure I liked and wasn't going to dwell on now. I wasn't up for that kind of emotional rollercoaster.

"It is, but it's also cemented. I really am sorry, Joilyn. I would never have hurt you on purpose."

"We were going to be married, Jacob. Be together forever."

"You *died*. You fuckin' *died*!" That came out harsher than I wanted it to, but I felt guilty enough without this. "I know I let you down, OK? It seems to be my superpower. I'll help you in any way I can. I'll make sure you have a safe place among people you can trust. I'll have Lemon get someone at Grim to assess your skills and vouch for you with ExFil, if that's what you want. Maybe Scout can help with that since he knows you. I'll do everything I can to help you. But I love Gina."

"Didn't you love me once too? Doesn't our past count for something?" She stood and crossed to me, putting her hand on my chest.

I caught her wrists and gently put her at arm's length. "Don't, Joilyn. I'm not yours to touch."

"You should be, though," she said softly. "You said when you left we'd get married when you came home. I thought I'd have time to finish my service before you were out, then we'd have more in common."

I narrowed my eyes. This wasn't… this wasn't the Joilyn I knew. Sure, we'd both changed, but I was getting whiplash with her emotional swings. "You knew going in it was a one-way trip. Why are you upset now?"

She shrugged. "Maybe because the man I love found another woman?" Now she looked angry. "Look. I get you needed to have a fling. I did too. But we can be back together now. Besides, I had you first. I should get to say if you stay with me or not."

"What's wrong with you, Joi? Not only are you

not making any sense, you've set down some very unreasonable expectations."

Taking a step toward me she reached out once more. Slowly this time until she lay one hand on my chest over my heart. "I just want us to be a team, Jacob." She looked at the door once and took another half step forward, lowering her voice like she was afraid someone would overhear us. "Listen. If you come back with me, we can work together. We'd be unstoppable. Just think of all the good we could do. Together."

"Is that what this is about?" I straightened from the desk, forcing her to take a step backward before she realized she was giving ground. "To get me back in the CIA?"

"Why not? They said you were good. And, like I said, we could work together. Me, you, maybe even Rattler. It'd be like old times." It hadn't missed my notice that her tears had dried. I wasn't delving too deep here because I honestly didn't want to know. Instead, I make a mental note to tell Lemon not to let her anywhere near the Grim Road compound and have a talk with Rattler about my suspicions. I had no doubt now what had happened, and it involved the CIA getting someone inside Grim Road to get an idea of how many of us and exactly who was there. After all, most of us had been affiliated with the CIA in some form, especially once we started running black ops.

"No. It won't." I moved around her to the door, intending to leave.

"I still love you, Falcon." She stated the words with such conviction, I couldn't tell if it was an act or not. "I always will. I'm willing to die for you."

I shut the door with a hard thud before advancing on Joilyn. "Is that a threat?" I bared my teeth at her and she recoiled. But, again, I saw something in her eyes that said she wasn't at all intimidated by me.

"What? That I'd kill myself? You can rest assured I'd never take my own life, Falcon."

"No. I don't think you would. But that wasn't the threat. The threat was in what you didn't say. You're willing to die for me. But I'm also betting you're willing to kill."

She shrugged. "Dying's much harder than killing."

"Oh, dying can most certainly be harder than killing. Especially if you hurt someone who belongs to me. I'm going to pretend I don't know what your assignment is. But don't expect to get into Grim Road. You'll have to figure something else out."

That drew what seemed to be a genuinely shocked expression from her. "What?"

"I'll go tell your… *handler* you're not getting into Grim Road and to make some other arrangements for you."

"You said you'd help me."

"And I will. But living at Grim Road is not on the table." Once again, I turned to go. I needed to think about what I was going to do next. Which meant staying longer than I'd planned at Salvation's Bane. I needed to get in touch with Lemon. Tell her what was going on. But most of all, I needed her to bring Gina with her. I absolutely could not spend another night away from her. "Joilyn? If you can get out of the CIA, you need to do it now. Scout said he didn't tell them, but I'm betting you told them. They told you to use Scout to get inside Grim Road. If you want out, Scout can help you. But you're not getting into Grim Road, whether you leave them or not. You might want to consider making the appropriate apology to Scout so you at least have the option of exiting the agency for real this time. Before they have you doing things you can't come back from."

Chapter Nine

Gina

Falcon texted me to let me know he was good and on a plane heading home. I wanted to call him but figured he'd reach out to me if he could. Since I had no idea what was involved with calling home when he was on an assignment, I didn't know the protocol. I couldn't help but constantly look out the window, hoping to see him coming home. True to her word, Lemon didn't leave my side for the entire three days since Falcon had left.

It had now been several hours since I'd gotten that text and no word. I was starting to get worried. What if something had happened to him?

"Rocket says everything's fine." Lemon read the message from her phone. "He said they were meeting at Salvation's Bane and he'll be by to get us in a bit."

"You mean, leave the compound?" My heart rate sped up. I wasn't sure I was ready for that. I heard the women talk. Falcon was pretty popular. Seeing one of them touch him, or having them compete for his attention might break me at this point. I'd latched on to him, even believing he would eventually break my heart.

"No one's gonna hurt you, you know." Lemon spoke gently, covering my hand with hers and squeezing lightly. Lemon wasn't overly demonstrative toward others, but she did offer affection when she considered it necessary. "I won't let them."

"You're not much older than me, Lemon. How do you wield so much power so effortlessly?"

She gave me an almost evil smile. "I sacrifice the genitals of all the men whose balls I've busted. Highly recommend it. Keeps a happy home." I couldn't help but laugh. Whatever happened after all this, I would always be grateful for Lemon's friendship.

There was a rumbling of a vehicle outside the house and Lemon stood, tugging me to my feet. "That's Rocket. He's takin' us to the Bane compound. Knox and Bear are following us so we'll have room to bring home Falcon and Rattler."

I glanced around the room. Cecilia and Olivia were here now. The others had been rotating sitting with me and Lemon. Also, the kids had been over during the day. We'd made and eaten so many cookies I was afraid they might turn into one. Lemon had told me numerous times she wanted Grim Road to be a home. Well, as far as I was concerned, she'd succeeded in spades.

We rode in silence. I was too nervous to carry on a conversation, but it only took us twenty minutes to get there anyway. By the time we rolled inside the chain-link fence I really thought I was going to throw up.

There were several people outside, talking, drinking beer, smoking. They appeared somber, but friendly.

"Give them a minute." A man with the title "President" and the name "Thorn" approached us. He'd just come from inside.

"Everything OK?" Lemon asked softly.

"I think so." Thorn shrugged. "Suffice it to say, they all have things to work out."

"Fuck you, Jacob!" An irate-looking woman stomped out of the building. "I didn't do anything the two of you didn't do! I just had to disappear for a little while! Tell me you didn't do the same thing, then come talk to me about the future." She stabbed a finger in the direction of the door just as Falcon and Rattler followed her out.

"Look, I'm sorry," Falcon called after her. "I'll help you with whatever you need."

"I *need* my fiancé and my brother to support me in my career!" As Falcon got close, she lunged into him and shoved his chest hard. Falcon didn't budge, but he didn't reach for her like I thought he might. "I did what I did because the Marines and the CIA told me I had exceptional talent. If you can't deal with that, maybe I don't need you in my life, even if I still want you!"

"Joilyn, you left us." Rattler reached for his sister but she batted at his hands, stepping further away from him. "We both thought you were dead. Why didn't you at least tell us what was going on?" Rattler still held out his hand, pleading with his sister. "It's been three years. How were we supposed to know you were undercover?" Both men were focused squarely on Joilyn. I doubt they even realized they had an audience.

I winced. "This was a bad idea. Maybe I should go." My voice was tight as my throat closed up. I'd expected this, but it still hurt. Someone put a hand on my shoulder and turned me around, pulling me into their arms for a tight hug. It took a moment to realize it was Lemon.

"I-I sh-shouldn't be h-here. I w-want to g-go h-home." The next thing I knew, I was surrounded by the men from Grim Road and Venus. She and Piston were regulars in the Grim Road compound, though Venus was actually a member of Salvation's Bane. I'd heard they'd been given memberships into several clubs and now acted kind of like ambassadors or mediators or something for all the clubs Grim was active with.

"Come on, little one," Venus murmured to me.

Lemon passed me off to the other woman. Venus and Piston urged me away from the clubhouse. I hadn't even gone inside. "It will be all right."

"I d-don't know why I c-came." I tried to keep my voice steady, but wasn't sure how well I managed it. "This was a s-stupid idea."

"Was not," Piston said gruffly. "Seems to me someone is regretting her life choices and taking it out on the people who love her. Don't worry. Your man's not letting her manipulate him."

"I can't --" I sucked in a breath. "I can't w-watch this."

Venus wrapped an arm around me while Piston led the way back to the garage. When I stumbled, Piston grunted, but scooped me up into his arms and strode into the building. Venus said something and Piston grunted again.

"I'll sit with her. You go make sure Falcon doesn't have his head up his ass." Piston had set me on a bench and Venus sat beside me, her arm going around me and pulling me to her.

"He's good. I'm more worried about Joilyn. I don't think she's mentally stable."

Piston turned and jogged out of the garage and I was left with Venus. She still had her arms around me, patting me like a mother might an upset child.

"I'm sorry. I'm sorry."

"No reason for you to apologize," Venus reassured me in her soft Russian accent. "Falcon messaged Lemon to bring you to Salvation's Bane. He wanted you here, Gina. Don't give up on him."

"H-He did?" I hated that I looked up at Venus with the hope that suddenly blossomed in me, but I couldn't help it. I wanted Falcon. I wanted him to be my own. I… I loved him.

"He did. He knew Joilyn was coming home and he still chose you."

"He d-didn't even l-look at me."

"He will." Venus continued with the comforting arm around me, while she stroked my hair with the other. I was ashamed to admit how hard I clung to her.

"I never used to be this clingy," I admitted to Venus as I desperately tried to get myself under control. "Never had anyone to cling to."

"And that's shame, little sister." Venus didn't let me go, but continued to comfort me when I felt like I was going to shatter. "You should have always have had someone to cling to when you hurt."

I'd just started to calm down when I heard raised voices outside and getting closer. I cringed, shrinking back. Venus let me go, but didn't move away completely.

"You're being unreasonable, Joilyn. You can't expect Falcon to just pick up where you two left off. He's not the same person he was and neither are you." Falcon and Rattler entered the garage with Joilyn, who bristled with anger, her back ramrod straight.

"It hasn't been that long!" Joilyn argued back.

"Three. *Three years*, Joi. Three years where he went through just as much hell as you did. We both did. Not just from the night that fuckin' mission went to shit, but from your *death*." Rattler crossed his arms over his chest and stood between Joilyn and the exit. Though the smaller door where Rattler stood open, the larger bays were closed.

"I was in a military compound, Ruben! Doing my part to stop domestic terrorism. I was cut off from everyone and everything!"

"You got word to your handler. He could have gotten word to me. Or Falcon?"

She shrugged. "I was on a mission. One that went to shit and back. I didn't have time to give him a list of people to contact."

"You were told when you entered the program you'd be severing ties with everyone, Joilyn." Another man entered the garage, but from inside the main clubhouse. "You knew there was no going back."

"I can't believe you let her do this, Scout," Rattler snapped. "How the fuck did you end up being her handler, huh? You recruited her, didn't you?" Rattler was furious. He was up in Scout's face, yelling at the other man.

Scout raised his hands and took a step back. "Hey, Rattler. Ease up, man. I inherited Joilyn from the woman who recruited her." Scout tilted his head. "No, actually, that's not true. I found out Joilyn was your sister and I bullied my way into being her handler. It's part of the reason she didn't fully trust me. She and I hadn't been working together that long before they imbedded her."

"Why didn't you pull her the fuck out?" Rattler stepped even closer to Scout and I knew the two were likely going to come to blows.

"You think I didn't want to? She was perfect for what they needed. They shaped her specifically for these kinds of infiltrations. They weren't letting her go for any reason. They needed her right where she was."

"They same as got her killed, Scout. If you're not lying, they think she's dead."

Scout's mien hardened. "You don't believe me? Talk to Cain. I don't keep secrets from Cain, especially if they affect ExFil."

"Ease up, man." Falcon had come up behind Rattler and gripped his shoulder. "He did what he could to help Joilyn. Ultimately, he's responsible for getting her out. Killin' him would be a shit way to say thanks."

I trembled where I stood. Venus was still with me. I had no idea when I'd moved closer to the small group and I knew it was rude to eavesdrop, but all I could see was Falcon. I needed to touch him. To have him hold me. I knew I couldn't interrupt, but I needed to know he was really OK.

He glanced over, his gaze capturing mine in an instant as though he could feel my desperate need for reassurance. Our eyes met across the tension-filled room, and something in his expression softened. He excused himself from the heated discussion and walked toward me, his steps determined yet gentle.

As Falcon approached, Venus subtly shifted aside, giving us space. My heart raced as he stopped in front of me, his large hands reaching out to gently cup my face. "Gina," he murmured, voice thick with emotion. "I'm so sorry. I should never have left you for this. Scout and ExFil had it covered."

I couldn't speak. The words were lodged somewhere deep within my throat, choked by tears and relief. Instead, I leaned into him, closing the gap between us. His arms enveloped me in a protective embrace, a haven from the storm swirling around us. The warmth of his body was a solid reminder that he was real, alive, and here with me.

"I was so scared," I admitted into Falcon's chest, my voice muffled by his leather jacket. "Were you hurt?"

"No, baby. Not a scratch. I swear."

I wasn't sure how to ask the next question, but I figured it was better to just get it out as quickly as I could. I took a breath. "Are you going back to her? I mean, I understand. You were supposed to get married."

"Gina, no. We'll talk about it all later, but no. Even if you weren't my woman, I wouldn't go back to Joilyn. She made her choices and they didn't include being my wife."

"I'm so sorry, Falcon."

"Don't be, honey. Joilyn and I would never have worked together. Not in the long run. Besides, I much prefer the woman I have now."

"I'm broken." I shook my head as I looked up at him. I felt so helpless. The only time in my life I hadn't felt helpless was when I was in his arms. "I'm not sure I'll ever be whole."

"That's a good thing. Because I'm broken too. Maybe if we stick together, we can complete each other."

Chapter Ten

Falcon

The second my gaze landed on Gina's sweet face, I thought maybe I'd finally done something right. The second I wrapped my arms around her, I knew with absolute certainty I'd come home.

I held her tightly, burying my face in her hair. It probably made me look weak to clutch her so tightly, but I didn't care. It wasn't like I was ever going to be an officer in Grim Road. They were my brothers and knew I'd defend them to the death. Who gave a fuck what another club thought?

"Thank you for coming, baby. I know it was hard for you. I just wasn't sure how long we were going to have to stay here before going back to Grim Road and I didn't think I could wait even a couple of hours to see you." It was the fucking truth.

"I was afraid. But I couldn't not come."

"Afraid for your safety?" I could understand her fear, though I'd hoped she'd realized we would protect her as our own. She was one of us and we were learning to support each other. In fact, once Lemon had gotten started on us, we'd all taken to it like we would have if we'd had our own families in a normal world. Seemed we all wanted the same thing and just hadn't wanted to admit it to anyone.

"Oh, no! Not at all. I trust Lemon and Rocket. They wouldn't let me come if they thought there was danger."

"Then what, baby? What were you scared of?" I kissed her head, loving that she clung to me just as hard as I did her.

"Of losing you. I don't know what happened to her but I'm sure you still love her."

I thought about that. "I suppose I do, in a way. I knew her a long time before we ever got together." I sighed. "I haven't really had time to examine my feelings, but the one thing I'm absolutely certain of is, I want you, Gina."

She didn't say anything else, but I could feel her body shaking as she cried. I glanced over at Rattler. He and Scout hadn't come to blows yet, but judging by Rattler's expression, the jury was still out on how long a reprieve Scout got. But for now, it seemed they were going to be civil.

Gina stiffened in my arms and I turned my head. Joilyn was staring at us with hot anger. She looked from Gina back to me before giving me a disgusted look and leaving the garage. I didn't loosen my hold on Gina, even when she tried to push away.

"Stop. Don't fight me, Gina. Not now."

"Are you sure this is what you want? I get it if it's not. You were going to marry her. It's going to hurt if you leave no matter what, but if you're going to her, do it now. While I have people still willing to help me get through it."

"This isn't the right place for this conversation, but you need to know it's you for me. No one else. I will never willingly leave you, Gina. Not for Joilyn. Not for anyone for any reason."

"You've never lied to me."

I was finally able to let her go, but only to frame her face in my hands so I could make this as clear to her as I could. "And I'm not gonna start now, baby. I'm sure not startin' now."

Gina nodded, her eyes glistening with tears. A fragile smile began to curve her lips. "I know."

"Come on, Falcon." Piston gripped my shoulder. "Let's get the ladies home. You guys all need the rest. I know Gina will rest easier back home."

"Yeah. I shouldn't have insisted she come. It was stupid."

"Never stupid to want your girl, Falcon. I'm glad we were able to give you both a swift reunion."

I hated to let Joilyn down, but this woman was where I belonged. Wherever she went, so did I.

The ride back to the Grim Road compound took thirty minutes instead of the twenty it had taken Rocket before. Yeah. There was a reason they called him Rocket. And it was thirty minutes confined in a cage. The big Ford was spacious and nice, but I needed my bike.

I leaned over to whisper in Gina's ear. "After I make love to you for a couple days, I'm takin' you on a ride. A long one. Just you and me."

She smiled up at me. "I'd like that." Then she blushed. "Kinda looking more forward to the first part, though." Then she turned and buried her face against my arm in embarrassment.

I chuckled and kissed the top of her head. "Me too, baby. Me too."

Knox took me and Gina to her house instead of stopping at the clubhouse. I gave him a nod of thanks before helping Gina out and into the house.

I wasn't sure what I expected to happen when I got her home, but having the woman throw herself at me the second the door was shut wasn't it. And, sweet Jesus, I was grateful! She wrapped her arms and legs around me in a tight embrace and fused her mouth to mine. The second she did, it was fucking over.

As Gina's lips eagerly met mine, I returned her passion with equal fervor. It was as if we both had been starving for this connection and couldn't get enough of each other's taste or touch. Our mouths moved in perfect sync, exploring and claiming. She was every bit as aggressive as I needed her to be. It was a side of her I hadn't seen before. It made my need for her all the worse, knowing how much she must want this.

My hands slid down her back to cup her ass, squeezing and kneading. She moaned into the kiss, pushing herself even tighter against me.

My tongue danced playfully with hers before delving deeper, exploring her mouth as my free hand tangled in her hair. The soft strands felt like silk between my fingers as I crushed them in my fist, holding on tightly, afraid she might slip away. I could feel the heat of her pussy through both our jeans as she moved herself up and down the rigid length of my cock.

Breaking the kiss reluctantly, I stared at Gina with what I knew had to be a ravenous, fevered gleam in my eyes. "God damn it," I whispered hoarsely, "I want you so fucking bad." She nodded and I was surprised to find that same feral desire reflected back in her eyes as she looked into mine.

"Yes. Please."

"You'll tell me if I hurt or scare you?" I have no idea where I found the presence of mind to say the words, let alone how I'd act if she needed to pull back. The lust that'd hit me the second she'd jumped into my arms wasn't altogether unexpected, but it was fucking strong! Primal. This was me and Gina. Claiming each other.

I trailed kisses down her supple neck to her collarbone before moving lower still. Nipping at her soft skin lightly, I continuing to explore what I could reach with my lips and tongue while I let my hands roam underneath her shirt to stroke and squeeze one perfect tit.

Gina arched her neck, giving me all the access I wanted to her creamy skin. Until it simply wasn't enough.

"Need you naked," I bit out in a hoarse demand. "Fuck!"

Immediately, she wiggled until she peeled her shirt off and whipped it over her head. My fingers found the back clasp to her bra and unfastened it with a flick so she could pull the offending material away from her chest and let it flutter to the floor.

I set her back on her feet so I could take off my own shirt. She stood there, bare-breasted with hints of moonlight filtering over her body. She was small but curvy in all the right places. Just like I remembered. Only this time, she was all mine. Forever. No one was ever taking her away from me again. Not another brother. Not fucking Hammer. Not Joilyn. No one. Gina was mine and I would protect her with my life.

I had to stop myself from taking her to the floor and covering her body with my own. She deserved better than that. She deserved to be worshipped and loved until she couldn't remember her own name. And then, I'd do it all over again.

"Turn around," I commanded. She complied, turning her back to me and her hands against the wall so that my hot gaze could trace every ridge of her spine as she presented herself to me like the offering she truly was. God, she was fucking perfect! Every curve, every dip and swell just screamed *mine*! Mine alone.

I kissed and sucked on the soft skin of her neck and back, kissing and nipping down her spine. I slipped my hands underneath the waistband of her panties, sliding them down her thighs until they pooled on the floor at her feet.

I slid a finger to the inside of her thigh, moving my hand upward to her pussy and brushing against her slick folds. She gasped, arching into my touch with a needy moan. Fuck! She was already wet for me. My girl was so turned on, it nearly shattered me.

As I explored her folds further I pushed my fingers inside to feel how wet and ready she was for me. She clenched her pussy around each digit as if greedy for more. As if wanting my cock to fill her. Gina moaned loudly when I found her clit and began circling it gently with my thumb while continuing to stretch her pussy with my fingers, searching for that hidden spot inside her to send her soaring.

The second I found it, she screamed, her pussy clamping down on my fingers. Sweat erupted over her skin and her knees gave out. I caught her, wrapping an arm around her waist to hold her steady while she rode out the orgasmic wave to its conclusion.

The second her body relaxed, I stood turning her in my arms and picking her up so that she wrapped her legs around my waist and clung. I carried her to the bedroom and kicked the door shut on my way inside.

"Fuck," I growled against her neck as she wrapped her arms around me as tightly as her legs were. She latched on to my ear and little whimpers escaped as she licked and nuzzled me. "So fuckin' hot. So fuckin' sweet."

"Please, Falcon," she whimpered. "Oh, God, please!"

"You need me, baby?"

"I do." She clung to me, even when I laid her down. Her arms tightened around my neck and she found my lips with hers again.

"I gotta get my fuckin' pants off." I reached

between us to unfasten my fly and free my cock.

Gina let go of my neck to shove her hands between us, knocking into mine in her haste. She finally settled on shoving my jeans and briefs over my hips under my ass. She'd spread her legs wide, welcoming me when the head of my dick kissed her entrance.

Gina gasped and shuddered as my cock finally penetrated her tight, wet folds. She cried out, wincing as if in pain, but her nails dug into my ass and pulled me forward, welcoming me inside her body.

"Tell me you want to be mine," I whispered harshly as I fisted my hand in her hair, forcing her gaze up to mine. "Tell me you want this."

"I do! I need it so bad!"

"My cock? Or my ownership?"

Bless her, she didn't hesitate. "Both! I need both, Falcon!"

Nothing could compete with the primal need that pulsed through my body. I let out a low groan as I slowly filled her up, making sure to go slow despite the burning desire to take her right now. I kissed her deeply, savoring the reunion and our first time together since her dark days.

"Falcon," she gasped, looking up at me in wonder. "It's you." She cupped my face in her hands. There was a feverish gleam in her eyes as if she were riding a high. "It's always been... you." Her body relaxed and a dreamy smile spread her lips. "From the very first time we made love... It's always been you."

Her stark revelation filled me with something I had no hope of reining in. Pride? Possession? Protectiveness? All of it maybe. It also brought back the first time I ever saw her. I'd taken Hammer up on his offer to fuck his woman, not because I was into that kind of kinky shit, but because I wanted Gina like I'd never wanted another woman. I'd spent the entire night, not fucking her, but making love to her. I'd brought her as much pleasure as I could as often as I could. Leaving her that morning had hurt me worse than anything ever had. It had also brought back memories of leaving Joilyn. I hadn't acknowledged it then, but now I could admit I hadn't felt near the sense of loss when I'd left Joilyn as I did leaving Gina. Not that I didn't love Joilyn, I did. Just not to this degree. And if there had been any doubt up to this point if I made the right decision to stay with Gina or honor a promise I made to Joilyn before she let me think she'd died, it was erased the second I was seated fully inside her, looking down into those glittering copper-colored eyes of hers. Gina was my one. My only.

Her walls clenched around me, trying to keep me inside her as I began to move. Her hips rocked against me, meeting each thrust with one of her own. It felt so right, so natural. She wrapped her legs around me tighter, pulling me closer, deeper inside her, as she arched into every stroke. I roamed my hands over her body, tracing every inch of skin I could reach as I pumped into her. Her own fingers tangled in my hair and held on tightly as I kissed her, licking inside her mouth, eager for more of her delicious taste.

"I love you," she whimpered between kisses and cries. "I need you to know how much I love you. How m-much you m-mean to me." Her voice caught on her words as I continued to ride her tender body, needing to brand her with my seed like I needed to breathe.

As we moved together, the sweat dripped from my face and landed in the hollow of her throat. I watched in fascination as her eyes were closed as she cried out in bliss.

The smell of sex and desire filled the small room as we climaxed together. Gina jerked in my arms and my hips snapped against hers as I fucked her through our orgasms. Then I collapsed on top of her, my cock still embedded deeply inside her.

Chapter Eleven

Gina

I awoke with a heavy weight over my torso. It took me a moment to feel my way through the murk of sleep, but the masculine grunt at my back pulled me the rest of the way from sleep.

It was still full dark outside and the only light filtered through the blinds from the full moon outside. I turned my head slowly, looking over my shoulder. When I did, the arm tightened around me and another grunt sounded.

I smiled. Falcon was going to be a handful. I had the feeling he'd take over my life if I let him. And, honestly, I didn't care if he did as long as he was with me.

His cock stirred where it nestled between my ass cheeks, pulsing as it grew. Probably the beginning of morning wood, but I still giggled. Raising my leg, I reached between us and guided his cock to my entrance. He thrust and groaned while I sighed in happiness.

"Good mornin' to you too, darlin'," he rasped at my ear.

"I forgot where I was," I said, giving him a soft smile. "But I wasn't afraid. I knew you'd always be there."

"God, baby. What the fuck you do to me..." His cock throbbed inside me going from what I thought was probably pleasantly aroused to pulsing with need the second the words were out of my mouth.

Falcon thrust his hips, fucking me with long, sure strokes.

Gripping the sheets, I arched my back and moaned softly at the feeling of his hard length pushing inside my entrance only to retreat and start over again. My pussy was still tender from the previous night's passion but I craved more. More pleasure. More of him. More... *everything*!

As he began to move, I couldn't help but match his rhythm, our bodies sliding together in perfect harmony. His breathing grew heavier as he increased the pace, his hands gripping my hips tightly. I loved how forceful he was with me, yet always conscious of his considerable strength. And Falcon was most definitely strong. Roped with muscle from top to bottom, he was powerful, knowing how to use the muscle he possessed. I'd always thought his body a work of art, more so because he could be gentle with his instead of always deadly.

The friction between us sent sparks of pleasure coursing through my body, making me gasp for air. He kissed my neck softly, his stubble scratching against my sensitive skin, sending shivers down my spine. The scent of our sweat mixed with sex only intensified my arousal.

My fingers curled into the sheets as he pressed me deeper into the mattress beneath us. My cries and Falcon's grunts echoed off the walls, filling the room with erotic sounds that made it harder for me to think straight.

"Fuck," Falcon groaned, "I could do this all fuckin' day."

His words sent a wave of heat straight to my clit. "Yes," I breathed out between pants. "Let's do that."

He leaned down and captured my lips in a fierce kiss that left me breathless. His tongue danced with mine, exploring every inch he could reach and giving me another devastating kiss.

"Come with me, Gina," he bit out. "Fuckin' come

now!"

I screamed as Falcon shuddered above me, giving a helpless grunt. Hot seed poured into me and I pushed back against him, trying to get him to go deeper inside me so his cum could never leave my body.

When the storm ebbed and my energy was spent, I let my body go limp in his arms. Falcon rolled off me and, with a brief kiss to my forehead, went to the bathroom. I assumed to clean up and wondered if I should follow him.

I'd just started to sit up when he came back to the bedroom with a wet cloth. "Lie back, baby. Let me wash you."

"You don't have to do that."

"I know. I want to."

Watching him closely, I parted my legs. He lowered the cloth to my pussy and gently washed my swollen flesh and the insides of my thighs. Then he leaned down and kissed my mound gently. I sucked in a breath as he rose and winked at me.

"Wicked man," I muttered.

"Heard that," he called back.

I couldn't help but giggle. This was the Falcon I knew and wanted. He was intense but playful and so very protective. I'd known he was the real deal the first time I met him. Every time after that he came to me, he only reinforced my belief that he was a very, very good man. I wanted that man for my own.

"I love you, Falcon." I looked up at him to meet his gaze. I needed him to know I meant what I said. I wasn't just saying this because I thought it was what he wanted to hear or to make him feel obligated to stay with me. It was the honest truth. "I want you to be happy. Whatever you choose. That's all I want for you."

He raised an eyebrow. "And what about you? Don't you deserve to be happy?"

"Well, yeah. But not at the expense of a good man like you. I won't lie. It'll hurt like hell. But you deserve a chance at the life that got taken from you. If that's what you want."

"Well, lucky for me, that's not what I want." He leaned down and kissed me again. Lightly, but no less passionately. "You're stuck with me, honey. And I don't want to hear another word about it."

He settled into bed with me again. I lay cuddled against his chest, swirling my fingers through the sparse hair beneath them. "What happened, Falcon? With Joilyn. Before and… on the way home. I know you had to have talked to her."

Falcon sighed and kissed me again. It seemed like a compulsion with him, like he had things to say, but got sidetracked. I couldn't deny I loved it. Even if he was trying to distract me.

"Baby, are you sure you want to talk about this? I'm here with you. I'm not going anywhere, not even for her. I don't want you to be upset because there's no reason for it."

"She wants you back, doesn't she?"

"It doesn't matter what she wants, baby. She chose her path, still walks the same fuckin' path that led us here. What matters now is what I want. And I want *you*."

I blinked away the tears that threatened to spill. "And you're really, really sure about that?"

Falcon propped himself up on one elbow, looking down at me with those intense eyes that always seemed to peer right into my soul. "Gina, honey, I've never been more sure about anything in my life."

His declaration warmed me, chasing away the ghosts of doubt that lingered in the corners of my mind. With a deep breath, I let go of the last tendrils of insecurity and smiled up at him. "Then I'm all in, Falcon. No looking back."

He grinned that lopsided smile that had first drawn me to him. "That's my girl." He kissed me once more before settling back on his pillow, me firmly against his chest, and tugged the covers closer around us. "Get some rest, baby. I have a feeling tomorrow's gonna be a long day."

Chapter Twelve

Falcon

"Look, man. Believe me or not. But I'm telling you, Joilyn is working with the CIA to get inside Grim Road." We were outside the Salvation's Bane MC compound in a yard where they had parties with other clubs, or friends and family. Whatever the occasion. Rattler braced himself with his palms flat on the surface of a nearby picnic table and hung his head. I knew the feeling. While I didn't want to marry Joilyn anymore, that didn't mean I didn't still care about her. This whole other side to Joilyn was throwing me, but I thought there were still glimpses of the young woman I'd known and had thought I'd wanted to spend my life with.

"Did she admit to that?"

"She didn't have to, Rattler. She didn't even try to deny it. She wants the three of us to be a team. She doesn't understand they're manipulating her to get to us."

"Or maybe she knows and doesn't care." Rattler shook his head. "You know how that place is. They get you isolated from everyone and everything you've ever known, then make you rely on them. On your handler. Whoever they tell you to trust. Deep down, you know something's wrong, but you can't place it. Before you know it, you're a lifer. You're in that middle place where you're a true believer. Just far enough up the food chain to have some authority but not far enough to realize everything they do has three or four different agendas, each one acting like a cascade until the end is reached."

"Yeah," I said, throwing the toothpick I was chewing on to the ground. "And the end result is never anything you'd have agreed to if you'd known what was happening."

"Christ, what's she gotten herself into?"

I tilted my head to the side just as a man walked out of the clubhouse. Finally, a place to focus my anger. I lifted my chin in the man's direction. "Ask Scout."

Yeah. That might have been the exact wrong thing to say. Rattler pushed off from the table and stormed off toward Scout. The other man gave him a wary look that morphed into resignation. Then Rattler swung a haymaker at Scout's face, connecting with a *crunch*.

Scout grunted and blood spurted from his nose. I tensed, not sure if I would have to pull Rattler off Scout or help Rattler beat Scout to a bloody pulp. Could go either way.

"You son of a bitch!" Rattler bit out, getting up in the other man's face. "If I find out you had anything to do with this, I swear I'll fuckin' gut you!"

"It's exactly as I told you. When I figured out who she was and what they had her doing, I did my best to intervene. But they already had her part way in and I didn't even talk to her until a couple weeks before she was fully embedded. That was all the time I had and she didn't trust me yet. She wasn't gonna take my word over the people she'd been training with for a year." Scout brushed at the blood dripping steadily from his nose with the back of his arm. "All I could do was keep her as safe as possible on this end, wait for things to happen, and minimize the damage."

"You coulda pulled her out."

"You think I didn't try?" Scout spat blood and brushed at his nose again. The blood still leaked in a steady drip, but was slowing. "I tried to get them to stop the raid when she called it in. Children in the compound we hadn't planned on being there should have been enough to at least delay the start."

"Why didn't they?"

"Because whatever their ultimate goal, they deemed it more important. And no, I don't know what the goal is, but staging this scale of an exercise tells me it's not something I want to even contemplate where anyone can hear me."

"And when everyone realized the place was on alert?"

"Again, I tried. I went so far as to disobey direct orders and got myself physically restrained. Then, after, Joilyn went dark. I got reassigned. Only, I kept an eye on the compound and established Joilyn was still there."

"And you didn't tell anyone? That she was alive?" I could tell Rattler was still pissed and I wasn't sure if Scout's explanation was helping or hurting.

"No. I had no idea what they'd do, but I knew they wouldn't want to take a chance she'd blow the whistle on a covert CIA operation in fucking Oklahoma."

"So you just waited. Hoping she'd contact you."

"No, Rattler. I didn't just wait. I contacted her. I let her know I wasn't working through official CIA channels and that our connection was secure if she decided to trust me. It was weeks before she even acknowledged the message. When she did, she only said, 'Acknowledged.' All I could do was wait."

"Christ." Rattler scrubbed a hand over his face. I knew the feeling.

"This is way the fuck above my paygrade." I pointed at Scout. "And fuck you anyway. You're good in a fight, Scout. Why you workin' for the spooks?"

"I have my reasons. But mostly it's to find the agents they left behind. Those men and women belong at Grim Road, Falcon. Joilyn does too."

"Not until I can be certain she's on the up and up." I shook my head. "Who's to say one of those cascading agendas didn't include you bringing her here? You may not even know it."

"Fuck!" Scout gave a rare display of temper. I'd only met the guy a couple of times, but I knew him by reputation. Word was he was always cool under fire, so for him to have this explosion of temper, no matter how mild, told me he hadn't thought of this. "Have I been leading them straight to former agents trying to hide?"

"We need to talk to Thorn here at Bane and Rocket at Grim." I pulled Rattler farther away from Scout, using the distraction to diffuse the situation as much as I could. "Joilyn has to have someplace to go until she figures out what she wants. It can't be Grim and I don't think Thorn'll want her here."

"I can find my own place to stay." The three of us turned to see Joilyn standing next to a palm tree in the yard. She was smoking a cigarette like she hadn't a care in the world.

"Joilyn, we'll figure it out." Rattler stepped toward her, but she flipped her cigarette aside and turned to leave. "Joilyn!"

"I don't need your help, Ruben," she called over her shoulder. "I know what I'm doing."

"Stop, Joilyn." Rattler followed his sister. "Just come back and let's talk."

"Nothing to talk about. I have my life and you guys have yours."

"There's no reason we can't all still be a family. I can help protect you, but you've gotta give me something."

"I don't have to give you anything, Ruben." Joilyn's voice was cold. Not at all like the woman I used to know. For the first time since she'd come back from the dead, I could see the real woman. The woman she'd become. "I had a job to do and I did it. Getting inside Grim Road was a pipe dream, but I was game to try." She threw us a grin over her shoulder. "So long, guys."

"Come on, Joi," Rattler yelled. "Come home. We'll figure it out."

"I *am* going home, Ruben." She glanced at me and I caught a glimpse of the woman I'd left behind when I went into the Marines. Then her expression morphed into one of complete indifference.

She took off at a jog away from the clubhouse and through the gate. No one stopped her leaving. Rattler looked torn, but also resigned.

"I can't just let my sister walk away, Falcon."

"You can't keep her if she don't want to stay, man."

"Christ," Rattler swore and took off after Joilyn.

She was safe. At least, as long as the agency didn't decide she was a loose end they needed to tie up. I pulled out my phone and shot off a text to Rattler. I'd support him with whatever he needed, but I couldn't follow Joilyn. She wasn't my problem and I had my own woman to worry about.

Chapter Thirteen

Gina

I saw Falcon and Rattler in the yard talking with Scout. Joilyn marched off and headed toward the gate. Rattler took off after her and I wanted to see what Falcon would do. I braced myself for him to join Rattler. If he did, I really thought my heart would break.

I took a breath and my heart pounded. Falcon turned to come back inside the clubhouse. He moved with purpose, his strides long and sure. The second he spotted me he hurried straight to me. I opened my arms and he wrapped his around me, crushing me to him.

"Honey, what are you doing out here? I thought you were asleep?"

"I missed you."

He urged my legs around his waist as he made his way through the clubhouse back to our room. The second the door was closed, he kissed me. It was frenzied at first and I thought I was in for a wild ride, but he gradually slowed things down. He laid me on the bed and covered my body with his, but simply settled between my legs before staring down at me and stroking my hair gently.

"I'm sorry, baby. This hasn't been easy on you. I'm sorry I've not been real… sharing. You know. With my feelings and shit."

I had to fight a grin as I blinked up at him. "Feelings and shit. You have feelings?"

"Brat," he grumbled, but grinned and leaned down to kiss me again. "I have feelings."

"Oh yeah? What kind?" I was probably setting myself up for heartache, but I couldn't help but push him a little.

"You know. The kind where I can't bear to let you out of my sight."

"So, you've got an obsession. You gonna stalk me?"

"If you try to leave me, sure. I'll stalk you until I find you out by yourself, then I'll drag you back to Grim Road and tie you to my bed." The arrogant lift to his eyebrow said he fully believed he could accomplish that, but I could also see a bit of humor in his features.

"Tie me to your bed?" I raised an eyebrow at him but smiled just the same. "Is that supposed to make me feel threatened?"

"It's supposed to make you feel wanted. Desired." He kissed me gently, then whispered against my lips. "Loved."

I pushed him back slightly so I could look into his eyes. "What? What did you say, Falcon?"

He grinned at me. "Is it so hard to believe I love you, Gina?"

"You… you love me?" I sucked in breath after breath, hardly able to believe what he'd said.

"I do, baby. I love you so fuckin' much."

"Oh, Falcon! I love you too! I love you too!"

The kisses that followed built a lust so hot I thought it would combust. The man was great with his tongue. In several different ways.

Somehow, he managed to get both of us undressed. It was kind of a blur because I couldn't get past kissing him. I loved the way he tasted. And how the Christ he managed to drive me so high so quickly with nothing but his kiss was not something I wanted to look too deeply into. Mainly because why *should* I care? It felt fucking good and I loved Falcon with all my heart.

I was about to come when Falcon entered me with a swift, hard thrust. The world blurred and I could only focus where our bodies joined, and my orgasm threatened to overwhelm me. I lost myself in the intensity coursing through every nerve ending. Falcon's movements were precise, designed to evoke a whirlwind of sensations that bordered on overwhelming. He knew exactly how to make me forget everything but the here and now.

"Falcon," I gasped between breaths, clinging to him as if he were my lifeline. He slowed then, almost stopping, pulling back to look into my eyes.

"What is it, baby?" Falcon's voice was thick with emotion, his eyes searching mine for any sign of hesitation.

"Just… don't stop," I managed to whisper, feeling an unexplainable fear of losing this connection we'd found. I shouldn't have worried, though. Hadn't Falcon proven time and time again how much he cared about me? Maybe I hadn't seen it at first, but even when he'd had to confront his past, he had never wavered in his commitment to me. I could see that now. Sure, finding out Joilyn was still alive had thrown him, but wouldn't it anybody? He'd never made me feel like he regretted being with me. He'd only ever made me feel loved. Cared for. Like I mattered.

With a sharp cry, I came, sweat erupting over my body as I clung to Falcon.

"I've got you, baby. I've got you." His voice was hoarse, and he trembled just as much as I did. His cock pulsed hard inside me and I realized he'd come with me.

We clung together for a long while. Falcon collapsed on top of me, pinning me to the mattress. I loved his weight. I loved how much bigger he was than me. I just loved Falcon.

I wanted to drift off into a sated sleep, but I had questions I needed answered.

"Falcon?"

"Yeah, baby."

"What happens next?"

He shifted, turning his face into my neck and sucking gently on the skin he found there. "We sleep for a while. Make love again before going back to sleep. Then, tomorrow, we go home. Then hopefully repeat the making love part. Several times."

"Falcon…"

He chuckled. "I'm only partially kidding. The truth is, I'm not really sure. For us, we're going home. I mean, assuming you want to come back home with me to Grim Road. Right?"

"Where else would I go? I want to be wherever you are. But what about Joilyn? She needs a place to stay. I heard part of what you guys were talking about in the yard. You don't know if you can trust Joilyn. But what happens if the people she works for didn't want her to survive? Won't she be in danger?"

Falcon let out a slow breath. He took his time answering. I wasn't sure if it was because he was choosing his words or if he wasn't sure how to answer. "I don't know. Honestly, though? Yeah. I think she's in danger. Maybe not right away, but at some point she'll start to think for herself. When she does, she's going to be more trouble than she's worth to them."

"So, you're saying she might dodge a bullet now, but more will follow."

"Yeah." We lay in silence for a while, and I had very nearly dozed off this time. "I feel sorry for Joilyn, Gina. Not like I pity her or anything. I'm angry she let them talk her into joining the CIA, and I'm angry she either didn't think through all the ways their arrangement could go wrong or did and still went along with them. I feel bad for her, but she created this situation herself. The second they said anything about faking her death, she should have run in the other direction."

"Sounds like maybe she should have run long before that."

"She wanted to serve her country like me and Rattler. I can respect that, even if I wouldn't have wanted that life for her. I can't be sorry she chose to serve her country. I know how the agency works. They're experts at recruiting the right people for the right job. They obviously saw something in Joilyn they knew they could use. And they were right." He nuzzled my cheek and neck, the coarse hair of his beard tickling slightly. "Joilyn wants to be where she is, I think. Sure, she misses me and Rattler, but she's all about the job. Whether she'll grow to understand the politics and intrigues of the agency is something we'll just have to wait and see."

"What are you going to do?"

"Now, that's an easy question, baby. I'm gonna take you home and do all that stuff I mentioned before. Hopefully all day every day for a long time."

I smiled. "You know what? That sounds just about perfect."

Dominic (Grim Road MC 8)
A Bones MC Romance
Marteeka Karland

I'm sergeant at arms of Grim Road MC. When I decide a woman is mine? She's mine.

Annie -- I'm seriously starting to question my life choices. The truth is, even though I was practically homeless and living on a meal a day most of the time, I'm vastly better off now than I had been. Unfortunately, stubbornness doesn't pay for shelter. Or even food, if you can believe it. I have a job at a local diner, but it's still hard to survive. Which is how I find myself in a bikini contest. If I make it out of this situation, I'm never doing this again. Yet somehow I end up in bed with the most wicked, dangerous man I've ever met. And why does he call to me like nothing else ever has in my life?

Dominic -- I'm not a people person on the best of days, but somehow Lemon talked me into being a judge at a local bikini contest. I'm pretty sure she's just trying to get me laid. Too bad every woman here's young enough to be my daughter. I'm a protective guy by nature and have a bit of a soft spot for vulnerable women. Unfortunately, my protective instincts kick in when my co-judge gropes one of the contestants. The shock on the young woman's face and the panicked way she flees the stage prompts me to act without considering the consequences... and that's how the fight starts...

Chapter One

Dominic

"I'm too old for this fuckin' shit." It was true too. At forty-eight years old I was definitely too old to be judging a bikini contest. Especially after as much beer as I'd consumed. Though I knew better than to touch without invitation, I was just as likely to say something equally offensive. But at least, maybe I wouldn't get myself arrested.

"Me too." The guy beside me was every bit my age and then some. He looked like the standard West Palm Beach retiree. Too much on the spray tan, too much on the hair transplants, and a little soft around the middle. He was also probably wealthy enough not to care about the going to jail part when he groped a young woman. Guy likely had a couple of the city's finest in his pocket in the case of something so trivial as touching a woman inappropriately without permission. Like in the middle of a bikini contest. Fucking bastard. "Don't mean I'm not enjoying every fucking second."

A huge smile on his face, the guy reached out -- just as I knew he would the second he'd sat down next to me at the judges' table -- and ran his hand up the inner thigh of one of the contestants. The girl sidestepped her way deftly out of reach and gave the guy a mock reproving look. Like it was all a big joke when I knew she'd reacted the way she had by pretending it hadn't bothered her that a strange man had been headed to the promised land without her permission. I'd always thought it was disgusting what women put up with sometimes. This was a prime example.

"No touching," I snapped at the guy. I was only

here because I'd let Lemon bully me into participating. Something about acting as security near the stage and looking good for the club in the community... Oh. And about me needing to get laid. Which, while I didn't disagree with her, I didn't want a child in my bed. These girls were all supposed to be at least eighteen but were young enough to be my daughters. I thought back to Tina and my own daughter, Calista. Calista was married to my enforcer and was probably about the same age as some of these girls. So, yeah. I knew grandparents who were my age. Tina was probably laughing at this whole situation from heaven. If she thought about me at all. I thought she might and I was determined to not do anything to make her ashamed of me. Which made this a colossal waste of time if Lemon was trying to get me hooked up. But I'd be Goddamned if I wouldn't put this guy in his place.

"Fuck you, man." The guy didn't even look at me. Instead, he reached for another woman walking past our table. This one obviously wasn't used to being in these sorts of things because she started when his hand slid up the back of her thigh to squeeze her ass before she could get out of his grip. She whipped around with a startled cry and the guy just laughed. "That's right, baby girl!" he yelled up at the young woman to be heard over the whoops and hollers. "Come to papa!"

The look on her face said she hadn't expected anything like this when she entered this contest and had no idea how to handle the situation. Which meant she'd probably either been tricked into entering, or she was desperate. I wasn't sure which to hope for, and I wasn't sure which made me more angry.

"Touch her again, I'll rip your arms off. You damn sure won't touch her after that." I actually bared my teeth. Which wasn't something I'd normally do. I prided myself on my cool head. I was methodical and planned each move as carefully as I could. I also listened to my instincts and factored them into my decisions. This time, however, I hadn't even thought about my move; I'd just acted, practically snarling like a rabid wolf. Also, I meant every single word. If he touched that girl again, I'd follow through with my promise.

"What the fuck, man? Why else would I be here if not to enjoy the show?" He gave me a cocky -- if a bit nervous-looking -- grin. "They all like it or they wouldn't put themselves in this kinda thing."

It took all my restraint not to wait until he touched the girl again -- and I knew he'd at least try -- and just beat the fuck outta him right now. "I'm not repeating myself. You've been warned."

"Fuck you." The guy sneered at me before reaching out to run his hand up the same girl's calf.

This time she jumped back, a panicked look on her face that sent a spike of fury through my chest. I reached out to the guy, fully intending to knock his hand off her. Instead, I grabbed the back of his head and shoved him face first into the edge of the stage. There was the crunch of bone, a spray of blood, and Mr. Handsy dropped to the ground and didn't move.

The girl on the stage gasped, slapping both hands over her mouth in shock. She looked from me to him and back before turning and fleeing the stage.

"Fuck." I hadn't meant to scare the girl and, for some fucking reason, it made my chest ache worse than my anger at imagined reasons for her being in this contest in the first Goddamned place.

All around me, men were still cheering, either not noticing the interaction between two of the judges or not caring. Keeping my eye on the fleeing girl so I could see exactly which way she went, I made note of the contestant number on her hip. I'd find out her name before I left this place, then I'd give that shit to Crush or Byte and they'd find her for me if needed. Oh, they'd moan and groan and tell me they needed more, after a bunch of grumbling and even more pizza, chips, dip, chicken wings, and anything else they could get Evelyn and Gina to make them. Which meant, I'd be bribing the women to make everything all in one go so I got my information faster.

Making my way through the crowd of horny men in their twenties, I headed in the direction I'd watched her leave. Still, no one said anything about the guy I'd just dropped. Were these fuckers for real?

Wait. Of course they were for real. I'd just answered that question when I'd made the judgment they were horny men in their twenties. Every ounce of blood flow that should have gone to their brains had likely gone straight to their dicks. Given the link between sex and violence, those guys wouldn't notice anything short of a bomb blast.

I hurried around the stage and saw her. Leaning against a concrete wall next to the women's bathroom. She had her hand over her stomach, and then she leaned forward and vomited.

"Sweet God above." Another woman emerged from the bathroom in a skimpy bikini like everyone else had on. She gave my girl a disgusted look, her tone of voice irritated in the extreme. "Girl, you've got to get a hold of yourself." She snickered. "If I curled up in a pile of puke every time someone grabbed me on stage, I'd never get through even one contest." She scrunched up her nose. "Not like you were ever going to win anyway." She flipped her hair over her shoulder, then twisted her ass toward the back of the stage. My girl sobbed as she finished vomiting.

I froze where I was as she fell back on her ass. She was half naked -- her bathing suit didn't cover much -- huddling on the ground in a protective ball as she cried.

"Girl? He hurt you?" I knew he hadn't, but I had no idea what her mindset was.

She shook her head but didn't say anything.

"Girl? Need a verbal answer." I stepped closer to her, careful not to spook her. I wasn't sure how long I had before someone realized Mr. Handsy at the judges' table was unconscious, or worse, and came looking for me.

"No." She wiped her mouth with the back of her hand and stood to her feet. "I just wasn't expecting anyone to touch me."

"He shouldn't have."

She looked up at me with large, hazel eyes. "You hurt him." She kept her voice low and her gaze shifted like she was looking for someone. "You should hurry and go. I don't want you to get into trouble."

"You don't... want... Girl, have you lost your mind?"

She gave me a confused look then shook her head. "Please just go. I can't lie for shit and if someone sees us together, they'll think I'm lying, no matter what, if I say I don't know you."

"What exactly are you afraid of here, girl?"

"That you'll get arrested? That I'll have to give a statement since I saw you shove his face into the stage and I can't lie and say I didn't see anything and I don't want to help get you arrested when all you were doing was being nice!" She said it all in one breath.

I had to stop myself from grinning. "Those are a

lot of fears."

"See? I'm a hot mess." Tears gathered in her eyes but she swallowed a couple of times and forced them back. Brave little thing.

"You're not a hot mess." I tried to be as gentle as I could. It was easy to see this girl was fragile. "You're just in an unfamiliar situation." Before I realized what I was doing, I reached out to brush a strand of hair away from her forehead. It was stuck in her eyelashes and I knew it had to be uncomfortable. She sucked in a breath, her lips parting.

Fuck.

Fuck!

What the fuck was I doing? Touching her? Why was every cell in my body suddenly focused on this girl? The last thing I wanted to do was get a fucking hard-on right now, but I was rapidly headed that way. "Sorry, sweetheart. I shouldn't have touched you."

"You made it better." Her eyes were wide, like she was shocked or something.

I tilted my head, trying to understand where she was going with this. "You're gonna have to explain that one, girl."

She shook her head, as if trying to snap out of whatever mindset she was in. "I-I mean, you weren't trying to hurt me or to touch me because you wanted to. You saw a strand of hair caught on my eyelashes and tried to make it better."

I frowned at her. "Girl? You all right?"

"What?" She gave me a confused look. "Yes! Yes. I'm fine. Look. I know I'm not acting right. I think it's a defense mechanism or something. I start saying what I'm thinking and my thought processes are kinda unusual sometimes." She closed her eyes and took a deep breath. "It all just gets jumbled because it all wants out at the same time or something. I promise I'm not daft. Just socially stunted. When I get nervous, that's what comes out."

"Honey, if you're that nervous about this, don't fuckin' do it. This thing ain't worth stressin' over."

"Yes. It is." She fluffed her hair and brushed the sand off her legs and hip where she'd sat on the sand-coated sidewalk.

"I don't know what the payout is, but it couldn't possibly be worth it."

"Every little bit helps." She winced but continued to brush the sand from her body in brisk motions. I'm ashamed to admit I imagined, ever so briefly, it was me brushing sand from her skin. I could practically feel what I was sure would be silky soft skin.

"How about let's get you dressed, so I can get you outta here. I think you've had enough for today." Could I sound any more like her father? Or a creeper?

"No! Wait!" She gave me a frantic look. "I have to get back on stage! I have to try!"

"Girl, do you honestly think you're gonna win after you took off like that? Besides I'm not going to hurt you. Just get you someplace less chaotic, so you can take a deep breath." The second I spoke I knew I'd fucked all the way up. You know. The first part. Not the last. Poor thing probably didn't even register the second part. Because I was a giant dick who'd just insulted her.

"No. I don't think I'm going to win. But if I'm not up there, I have exactly zero chance instead of a one percent chance of winning." With one more swipe at her mouth with the back of her hand, she stalked back toward the stage.

"Girl! Girl!" Of course, she didn't stop and there

was no way to keep from zeroing in on her ass. Which was... *a thing of fucking beauty.* How the hell had I missed such a beautiful, heart-shaped ass? The heels she wore flexed her calves and made the muscles in her legs play beneath her skin with every step.

The noise of the crowd was still loud and boisterous, the announcer cheerfully calling out names and various personal information about each contestant. I have no idea how anyone could hear anything over the crowd, but I don't think anyone really cared anyway. They were all about the near-naked women dancing across the stage, all vying for attention.

I knew I needed to let Lemon know her idea to get me laid went to shit, but I had bigger problems. Because when I looked at the stage all I could see was that same heart-shaped ass and those big hazel eyes. She wasn't as graceful as most of the women, nor as confident. Hell, she looked downright awkward, but she definitely had my attention. There was no way to even think about looking at another woman on that fucking stage.

I moved back to the judges' table where my co-judge was now back in his chair. Blood dripped steadily from his face but the bastard was still trying to grope the women on stage as they passed by.

"Why do some motherfuckers never fuckin' learn?" I muttered to myself. Stalking toward him, I clenched my fists. There was no way I'd get away clean twice so I was fully prepared to land my ass in jail when I reached his sorry ass because I was about to give him the beatdown of his motherfucking life.

He turned his head and his eyes widened when his gaze landed on me. The high-pitched squeal that came from the guy as he shoved up from the table and stumbled backward was a beautiful sound.

"Stay away from me! Stay away from me!" he yelled as he continued to try to keep distance between us. I had every intention of following him and continuing the beating but someone grasped my shoulder and shoved me back into my chair.

"You gotta pick the winner." Jimmy, the guy in charge of the whole mess gave me a frantic look. "Where'd the other judge go?"

I shrugged. "Ain't his keeper."

"Well, pick the winner so I can get the hell outta here. And there's a hundred bucks in it for you if you pick number twenty-five." His lips parted in a lascivious grin. "She promised to let me fuck her any way I wanted to if she won. Pretty cool what you can get a chick to do for money, huh?"

Jesus, this guy! It's people like him who made me want to go to the wild somewhere and disappear into nature. Just live off the land. No stupid-ass motherfuckers taking advantage of young women. Nothing to make an obviously socially awkward young woman enter a contest like this for whatever money it paid out.

I glanced at the judges' sheet, then back up at Jimmy. He gave me a grin, then turned and left the table.

"Hey, man." The announcer held his mic away from him so he could speak to me. He stood on the stage where he'd been moving down the line of girls, presenting them one last time. Now he looked ready to announce the winner. "Gimme the envelope."

I raised an eyebrow, then saw the envelope in question laying between me and where the other judge was supposed to be. I filled out the winner's sheet which consisted of a big number on a piece of paper, folded and stuffed it in the envelope. And no. I didn't pick number twenty-five.

"And this year's West Palm Beach Bikini Diva is…" Dramatic pause for effect. "Number fifty-eight! Annie Warren!" Aaaand I now had a name to go with the number.

Chapter Two

Annie

I stood there, not moving. The announcer called my name and I just stood there like an idiot! I won. And I couldn't seem to make myself move.

The guy stuck out his hand and I took it automatically. He tugged me to him, putting his hand around my waist and urging me to the front of the stage. I'm not even sure I was smiling. In fact, I probably looked terrified. My knees trembled and I wasn't sure how much longer I could walk in these Godforsaken heels without falling on my face.

Someone draped a sash around my body and handed me some cheap roses. Still, I stood there. Rooted to the spot.

"For fuck's sake, bitch. Wave and smile." The announcer bit out his order in an irritated voice, all the while smiling like he was the happiest person in the world.

I have no idea why I froze. Probably the encounter earlier. I definitely hadn't been expecting to win. Not in any way. Hadn't the man who'd come to my rescue said the same thing? No way I should have won after freaking out like I had. No matter the circumstances...

But wait. Wasn't that guy one of the judges? The other judge had been there when I'd first come back on stage -- bloody nose and eyes that were starting to bruise -- but was nowhere to be seen now. Only the other one. The guy from backstage. My hero.

He stood behind the judges' table, arms crossed over his chest with a satisfied smirk on his face. It was the first time I'd really gotten a good look at him. Sure, I'd been so close to him earlier I got a hit of the gasoline fumes clinging to him, but the scent hadn't really registered. Now, I noticed the black vest with patches. One side said "Dom," the other "SAA." Of course. A motorcycle gang or something. I'd seen a few at the diner, but they were all different from this guy. At least, they were at the diner. Most of them had women they simply doted on. Everyone seemed so happy. I hadn't believed it when Ulyana had told me about them when she'd convinced me to come with her. But I also knew from talking to her that not all clubs in the area were like the ones I saw at the diner. Stumbling into a guy who could quite possibly be on the wrong side of the law and dangerous to me sounded about right for my luck. Though, this guy hadn't seemed like the type to hurt me. In fact, he'd only been gentle. I couldn't imagine a man as dangerous and uncaring as people said bikers were would have taken the time to try to calm me down. Of course, he *had* also been a real jerk. There had been no reason to be mean about letting me know I wasn't going to win this contest.

Except I did win. And he'd obviously been the one who'd chosen me.

Behind me on the stage, there was an uproar. Women screeched and yelled. One in particular was very vocal.

"What the hell? Jimmy! You said I was gonna win!" a whiny, nasally voice piped up. I thought it was the same woman who'd made fun of me outside the bathroom.

"What?" This screech from another female voice. "How did you know you were gonna win? He literally *just* wrote the number on a piece of paper and stuffed it in an envelope. I watched him do it!"

"How could you possibly have given the win to

that little mouse?" That from the first woman.

"Are you saying this thing was rigged?" Voices called out from several different directions. Outrage and indignant denials came from all around me.

"Wait! Wait!" Another man jumped up on stage and grabbed the mic from the announcer. "You got it wrong. You didn't look at it right!" He tried to smile to cover his panic, whatever was happening, he was in a snit. "Gimmie that!" I thought the guy's name was Jimmy, the guy who'd organized the competition. He snatched the paper, envelope, and the mic from the announcer and looked at it, his smile widening. "Number twenty-five! Mercedes Golden!"

"Ten bucks says that's not her real name," I muttered as someone stripped off my sash and snatched the roses from me. I didn't care about the sash, and the roses sucked. I just wanted the money. And I was a tad bit snippy about it. It was right there in my hands! Ugh!

"Mercedes" acted like she'd won the Miss Universe contest instead of the West Palm Beach Bikini Diva contest. She blew kisses and waved her hand in front of her face like she was drying her tears. Well, until she was handed her check for a whole two hundred and fifty dollars. "What the fuck is this?" The woman looked outraged. "Where's the rest of the zeros?"

"I mean, if you don't want the check, I'll be happy to take it," I grumbled dryly. "What exactly were you expecting?"

Mercedes turned her venomous gaze on me and hissed. "Bitch."

"Me? What'd I do?" I knew I should just walk away. Let it go. For whatever reason my hero had tried to let me win, but I could have told him shit like that never worked out for me.

"You're *breathing*." Mercedes stepped close and gave me a hard shove. "Why don't you just shut up and *die*!"

I stumbled back and caught my high heel on… something, and tumbled to the floor on my ass. My view was a bit obscured after that because of my position on the stage, so I missed what exactly happened. When I finally got to my feet, there was a brawl on stage.

Mercedes slapped the piss outta Jimmy, and a couple of the other girls snagged Mercedes' hair and reached for the big check (Literally big. In size. Not dollar amount.) I have no idea why. It was one of those really huge trophy checks. It wasn't like it was actually good for anything. Right?

All around the stage, men and women hollered and cheered, wanting the fight to continue. Or, more accurately, wanting to introduce a kiddie pool full of Jell-O or pudding. Because, why the hell not?

Scooting backward, I tried to get out of the way and not get stepped on. Some of the women on the stage around me backed away, leaving the area, but more than a handful joined in the fight. It kind of looked like a battle royale.

Then, like some avenging angel, my hero pushed himself up onto the stage, his gaze quartering the area as if seeking a particular target. The second he spotted me, he got a determined expression on his face and stalked in my direction. He had to move several women aside and he did so carefully, obviously being mindful of his bigger size and greater strength.

Once he spotted me, his gaze never wavered. He moved straight to me without hesitation. When he reached me, he grabbed my hand and pulled me to my feet. Then he scooped me up and carried me through the throng of women on stage and the men climbing up to join them in the melee.

"Hang on, girl." His voice was warm and gruff. I shivered as I obeyed him, wrapping my arms tightly around his neck as he carried me to the end of the stage and shoved his way down the steps. When we reached the bottom, I fully expected him to set me on my feet, but he kept going, his long strides putting distance between us and the chaos behind us. "Where are your things?" His voice rumbled through me and I found myself clinging tighter, wanting to get closer to him. "Ain't got all day, girl. Answer."

I looked up at him and knew my eyes were wide as I took in his appearance. His hair was shaggy, but not too long. Kind of like he wanted it out of his way but had better shit to do than mess with his hair. There was a liberal amount of gray both in his hair and his beard. He was heavily muscled and I was pretty sure he was at least six inches taller than me. Or more. "Uh," I cleared my throat, trying to pull myself together and focus on what was going on around me. "I didn't bring much. It's strapped to my bike."

That got a grunt from him. "Didn't seem like the type, but makes this a whole lot easier." He sounded like he was talking to himself and not to me, so I didn't say anything. He still hadn't put me on my feet. "Where you parked?"

"Um, just over there?" I pointed to a nearby bicycle rack. "Mine's on the end."

He stopped and looked around like he couldn't see the bicycle rack only a few steps away. "Girl, ain't seein' no bikes anywhere."

"Really?" I rolled my eyes, squirming until he let me down, then walked over to where I'd left my bike.

It had a small pack strapped down to the back where I had a pair of shorts and a T-shirt.

"That ain't a fuckin' bike." He was right behind me. I could feel the heat from his body. OK, so it could have been heat from the afternoon sun, but I liked the thought of this man close to me. Yeah. I wasn't right in the head sometimes.

"Well, what do you call it?" I didn't turn around, preferring to pull on my clothes over my bikini without looking at the hunk of perfect, gruff man behind me.

"It's a fucking bicycle!" He sounded equal parts amused and frustrated, and like he wasn't sure which emotion would finally win out.

I shrugged. "Yeah. That's what I said. A bike."

"Sweetheart, there's a distinct difference between a bike and a bicycle."

I fastened my shorts and straightened my shirt as he spoke. I must have had a confused look on my face because he immediately frowned. He opened his mouth to speak, but I cut him off. "Look. I appreciate your help, but now I've got to go get a shower before my shift starts." I gave him what I hoped was a bright smile and waved as I pulled my bike out of the rack.

"Where the hell you think you're goin', girl?"

I blinked up at him as I straddled the seat and put my foot on the pedal to take off. "I just told you. I need a shower and I'm probably running a little late as it is. What time is it anyway?"

He tilted his head at me like he was curious. "Little after four."

I sucked in a breath. "After four?" My voice came out a little squeak. "Oh shit! I'm late! I'm so freaking late!" It took all I had not to burst into tears. "Marge told me if I was late she'd have to fire me! I can't lose that job!"

Putting all my weight into it, I stepped on the pedal of the bicycle... and nothing happened.

"Whoa there, girl. You can't go off ridin' that abomination in those fuckin' shoes."

"But I'm late!" I was starting to struggle now. Not physically. My insides felt icky. It was like when I got into trouble at the camp, only so much worse. At the camp I knew what the punishments were depending on the infraction. Out in the world? I didn't have a clue. Sure, Marge would fire me, but she was also the lady who owned the motel. Would she kick me out of my room too? Where would I sleep?

"Stop. You said Marge. You work at Tito's Diner?"

"Yes. I'm trying to learn to be on time. Marge says if I'm not, I'll get fired."

"OK. What time did your shift start?"

I could feel my lower lip trembling and I tried to bite it so I didn't lose my control on the stupid tears threatening. "Um, four o'clock." Could I sound any more miserable?

"Come on, girl." He held out a hand. I took it before I thought. "I'll get you there and see if I can smooth things over with Marge for you." It was ingrained in me to obey. The second I took his hand I realized I'd fallen back into the same trap I'd been in most of my life. Letting men in the camp dictate to me without so much as questioning them. It didn't matter how much I wanted to like this guy; I didn't know him. I was also pretty sure if I did know him, the last thing I'd do was take his hand.

I snatched my hand from his grasp and put both of my hands behind my back. "I'm fine," I said, looking down at my feet. "I just need to leave right now."

He sighed, long and loud, like I was the one putting him out. "Well, whatever you're gonna do, you should do it now. The crowd is thinnin' out, but I don't like you here by yourself."

I shrugged. "It's fine. I'll be fine."

"Uh-huh." He didn't sound convinced. "Look. I know Tito and Elena. Marge too. I'll ride on ahead and let them know what happened. It'll be all right." The guy looked uncomfortable with his offer of help and I wasn't sure why. Growing up in an encampment away from the real world had left me with more than a few social barriers. Sure, I'd learned to read people. Especially when they were angry. But the people on the outside were very different than what I'd been taught they were in the camp.

"I'm good. Honest." I gave him a bright smile. I stuck my shoes back into my bag and pulled out some flip-flops. Not the best for riding, but my hero was right. I couldn't very well make it to Tito's riding a bike in heels. "Thanks for your help. And for trying to let me win." I waved and smiled, then took off, doing my best not to let the familiar panic overtake me. "It was nice meeting you!" I called to him over my shoulder. Yeah. Not the best response. Sighing, I focused on my route ahead so I didn't get hurt because I didn't pay attention.

I wasn't very good at riding a bike. Until two weeks ago, I'd never done it. Leaving the camp had been more of a shock than I'd been prepared for. I supposed that's why all us kids had been kept isolated. So we'd be off balance and come running home if any of us ever decided to try to leave.

Keeping to the bike trail was hard. At least, for me it was. I was more than a little wobbly, but I kept on. If there was one thing I knew about myself, it was that I was stubborn. Too stubborn for my own good. My stubbornness was quite possibly the only positive thing I had going for me to keep me out of the camp and help me make a life for myself outside the hell I'd been living in.

Chapter Three

Annie

By the time I got to the diner, I knew I was in so much trouble. Not only was I not appropriately dressed, but I was sweating and still covered in the suntan oil the other candidates had slathered on them. Yeah. I was a hot mess.

I parked my bike next to the light pole in the back of the small parking lot out of the way of customers. Marge had told me to park next to the building on the corner, but there was a parking space there and I didn't want my bike to be in the way of anyone needing to walk on the sidewalk where I'd have to park.

There was a back entrance and that's where I went. That way, I could use the bathroom and freshen up quickly. I had a clean shirt and shorts in my locker as well as some underwear. Might seem a little odd, but I'd learned to always be prepared. If that meant I had to keep a backpack ready to go everywhere I had a hidey hole, that's what I'd do.

I hurried in, panic and worry squeezing my chest. Yeah. I knew I was in trouble. Thankfully, there was only one vehicle in the parking lot. A motorcycle. Which reminded me of my hero. Was that why he'd been confused about my bike? Because he rode one? Only a *real* one.

"Annie! There you are!" Elena met me at the bathroom door when I exited. I'd put my long brown hair into a bun at the back of my head. I hadn't been able to do much about all the suntan oil, but I'd washed as much as I could in the bathroom sink.

"I'm so sorry, Elena. I'll stay late and help with closing. I can even come in early tomorrow. Whatever you need." I was trembling, my stomach churning. Elena was the sweetest woman I'd ever met. She and Marge had taken a chance on me and given me a job. Marge had given me a room at the motel across the road at a discount. The very last thing I wanted to do was let either of them down.

"Relax, *preciosa*. It's fine. We were worried, is all." She gave me a reassuring smile. "You're still learning and that's fine. Marge and I promised to help you and we will. Now take a deep breath. Have you eaten today?"

"Yes." The answer was automatic. It was a lie, but I'd learned that people who asked that question were usually fulfilling a requirement. They didn't actually care. They just wanted it to seem like they did. I was really growing to love Elena and Marge. If I said that, no, I hadn't eaten, and she made light of it or told me to make sure I ate before I came to work, I'd probably shatter. It felt like I was holding myself together with spit and glue as it was.

Elena pursed her lips. "Everyone tells little white lies from time to time, *pequeña*, but you're no good at lying." She reached out and cupped my cheeks between her hands. "You will eat, *preciosa*. And not give me grief over feeding you, *sí*?"

"*Sí*, Elena." I took several deep breaths, trying to keep the tears back a little while longer. If I could get through eating in the back, where I was sure Elena would stay with me, I could get to work and not think about any of this. "*Prometo*." Elena and Tito were trying to teach me Spanish. I wasn't good yet, but I was picking up a few things. I practiced every chance I got because, if they were good enough to try to teach me, I wanted to make sure I gave it my all.

She had Tito make me a burger and fries while I

went back to the bathroom and did a little better job getting more of the suntan oil off my skin. I still felt like I stank, but I thought I smelled better than before I started. Progress!

When I came out of the bathroom, Elena was setting my plate down on the counter, pulling me up a chair. "Come. Sit." She smiled as she set a chocolate milkshake beside my plate.

"A milkshake too?" I couldn't help my smile. Of all the things I'd discovered after leaving the camp, Elena had just put in front of me my three favorites. Cheeseburgers, French fries, and ice cream. *Any* ice cream.

"Of course. Ice cream makes everything better." Her smile was so beautiful. The thing about Elena was her kindness. There wasn't a mean bone in her body. She was like everyone's mother. She knew her customers and their families. Those of us she employed? Well, she treated us like family.

There were only a couple of us. Tito, Marge, and Elena could easily run the place without me and Caroline, but I needed the job and Caroline was a people person. She was at her happiest during the lunch rush. I wasn't even sure she got paid. Or, rather, that she kept the pay Elena gave her. Caroline had told me her father was the doctor for a club called Salvation's Bane. If all the men and women in the clubs around the area were like the ones I'd met at Tito's, then I had no idea why MCs had such a bad rap.

Most of the time, I was pretty sure Caroline bought new clothing or food items for a homeless camp close to us. The people I'd met at Tito's had opened my eyes to so many things. Not the least of which was true compassion. Not submissive compassion either. These people weren't trying to gain anything, or get on someone's good side. They didn't care if people liked them or not. They did what they thought was right and treated people the way they wanted to be treated.

"Ice cream does make everything better." I grinned as I dug into the burger and fries.

"Is everything all right, *chica*?" Elena asked her question in a tender, caring voice. I could see the worry in her eyes.

"*Sí*, Elena. I'm *lo lamento* for being late. I promise to get a watch as soon as I can. I can probably get a kid's one for ten bucks or so. That's all I need. Right?" I hated that I sounded so unsure about something so simple. I also made a point to answer her with the few words of Spanish I'd remembered. Not trying to get on her good side or anything. I genuinely wanted to learn the language. I found that stress sometimes forced me to learn quicker than I normally would have. So I used at least some Spanish when I spoke to Elena or Tito, even when I was struggling with the current situation. Owning a watch was such a small thing, but I'd never owned one. Or anything else for that matter. In the camp, no one really owned anything. Well, other than the Divine One. I grinned as I dredged a crispy, golden fry through some ketchup and popped it in my mouth.

"There she is." Tito popped his head around the corner from the back, taking his place behind the counter where Elena had me eating. It wasn't the first time she'd done it, but it always took me by surprise.

I started to reply to Tito when the judge from the bikini contest followed him into the main part of the diner, moving to a seat next to me. I sucked in a breath... and nearly choked on a French fry.

"Easy, girl." His gruff voice went straight to my insides and heated them. What was wrong with me?

I'd never had these impulses before. Quite the opposite. I'd been doing everything I could since I'd turned sixteen to not be noticed by the men in the camp. Especially the Divine One. Now, for some reason, I really, *really* wanted this guy to notice me. I was also more than a little nervous of him. I might be simple and ignorant of life on the outside and how people truly interacted with each other, but I knew enough to know this was a man who would chew me up and spit me out. He was the type of man the Divine One would seek to make an ally because, otherwise, he'd be a threat.

"Sorry," I choked out. I coughed a couple of times. A glass of water was held under my nose and I took it gratefully. A few seconds later, I was fine. Elena rubbed and patted my back gently, like she might a child after they got something down the wrong way.

I probably should have taken a couple more seconds to get myself under control, but honestly, there was just no preparing for the effect this guy had on me. So I looked up at him before quickly lowering my gaze. It should be a sin for a man to look like he did, and I was certain everyone in the camp would tell me I was going to hell for sinful thoughts.

"Hey. No need to be sorry, girl. I'm sure you thought you'd never see me again. Though, to be fair, I did tell you I was comin' here to smooth things over with Marge. Remember?"

"Yeah."

"Her name's Annie, Dominic." Elena frowned at the big man. Wow. She was brave. I couldn't imagine anyone looking at this man that way and not peeing themselves when he focused his attention on them. "Not 'Girl'."

To my surprise, the big man looked

appropriately contrite. He ducked his head slightly, then winked at me. "I'm sorry, Annie. She's right. I never meant to insult you. I was simply trying to remind myself of our age difference." He said the last part with a wry grin, though I didn't really understand why.

"And that age difference is not something you will forget, *hombre*." Elena wagged her finger at Dominic, like she might chastise a child. Dominic merely gave Elena a sexy grin. "You know, our age difference isn't as big as mine and Annie's. What say you and me run off together, Elena? I'll treat you even better than Tito."

If anything, Elena scowled even more at Dominic. "You're charming, Dom. But you're not *that* charming. Besides, no one could treat me better than Tito. But you're welcome to try." She raised an eyebrow. "Just not with me." Elena glanced at me before smiling once more. "Take her to my office so she can finish eating in peace."

"Wait!" I called out to her, glancing from Elena to Dominic and back. "I need to... I mean, I'm sorry, Elena. You've been really good to me and I'm always messing up."

"Oh, *pequeña*." Her face softened as she gave me a warm and understanding look. "Everyone messes up. And you've had a lot thrown at you in a very short time. You're doing wonderfully and I'm so very proud of you for trying so hard." Elena reached over and took my hand and squeezed. "You are a precious, caring, and compassionate woman, Annie. You deserve to be happy." For some reason, Elena gave Dominic a hard, meaningful look. Like she'd just given him an order and expected to be obeyed. Dom narrowed his eyes, giving Elena a confused look back but said nothing.

"I need to get to work," I mumbled as I took one more bite of French fry. And ketchup. *Lots* of ketchup. Ketchup was the nectar of the gods!

"You'll come with me and finish your food," Dom said with a growl. He took my hand and led me back to Elena's office, then stood between me and the door and raised an eyebrow, daring me to challenge him.

My first impulse was to give in immediately, but the whole point of leaving the camp was to make my own decisions. For good or ill. I wanted to be my own person.

Instead of backing down, I put my shoulders back. "I'm finished." But I still reached for another fry. With ketchup. "And I've put Elena out enough today. The least I can do is get out there now and help her."

He stepped farther inside the door and shut it. Then he pointed at my food. "Sit. Eat."

"I don't have to do what you say." I was afraid I didn't sound nearly as confident as I needed to be. In fact, I was pretty sure there was a quaver in my voice.

Dominic's face softened. There was a hint of amusement in his face. "No, honey. You don't. But why cut your nose off to spite your face? You're hungry. Elena had Tito make you some dinner. Do you really want to waste his hard work?" He sounded so reasonable! And he had a point.

"No." I sank back into the chair in front of Elena's desk where she'd set my plate. "I'm sorry. You're right."

"Yes. I am." When I gave him an annoyed look, Dom winked at me again. Yeah. So in over my head it wasn't even funny. This guy could -- and would -- chew me up and spit me out if I let him get away with anything. "Eat." Grin. "Girl."

I huffed, giving him my best, most annoyed look, but I couldn't hold it. I started giggling, then just let it all out. What was the point in holding it all in? Hadn't I left so I could feel safe expressing myself when I felt the need? It felt good.

"Now, that's the sound I want to hear from you." Dominic nodded at my food before giving me a pointed look. "Eat up. I'll let Tito know you loved it so much you're eating every single bite."

Yep. I was definitely in trouble.

Chapter Four

Dominic

I left the little pixie alone to eat, gently closing the door behind me as I shut her in Elena's office. Elena came to me the second I poked my head out from the back into the main diner.

"You be good to that girl, Dom. She's got a lot going on."

I raised my hands, taking a step backward. "Whoa there, Elena. I'll be nice to her, but if you're thinking there's more going on, there ain't."

"Well, there should be." Elena stepped closer to me and wagged a finger in my face. "She could certainly do better than you, but you could never do better than her. That girl needs a strong man to protect her and show her she's worthy. When Venus brought her to me, I was thinking more about someone from Black Reign -- those boys are all good to their families -- but Grim Road might be a better fit with her... situation."

"And what's her situation?"

"That's not my story to tell. Just be gentle with her." Elena's expression softened, and she looked over my shoulder toward the back where Annie was, hopefully, finishing up her meal. Girl was so thin she could definitely use the calories. "She's extremely intelligent but a little... simple. She's lived her whole life in a completely different world, and she's only just broken free. At least physically." Elena gave me a sad smile. "She needs your protection."

I frowned. "And who's protecting her now?"

"That'd be me and Venus."

I turned at the sound of the declaration to find Piston sitting in a booth in the corner, away from the window and in full view of the room and every entrance and exit.

Piston had been a member of Grim Road a long fucking time. I thought he might have been a member longer than anyone alive. At least, in our region. Like the Iron Tzars, Grim Road MC had more than one club in more than one area of the country. Since most of the members had been some form of Black Ops at one time or another, they tended to want their privacy. We kept our club relatively small compared to other clubs, but with the addition of our women and children, we were growing out of our hidden compound. Piston and his woman, Venus, were newly appointed in a role resembling ambassadors for the club. They acted as liaisons for Grim Road, Black Reign, and Salvation's Bane MCs. The overall favorability of our clubs within the community and with each other had improved nicely.

"She in trouble?" I lingered by the entrance to the back, keeping myself between Annie and anyone in the diner. I'm not really sure why I felt the need, but there was no denying it. Fuck. This wasn't good.

"Eh, maybe. She left… an encampment. Call it a commune." He shrugged before continuing. "Venus thinks they'll leave her alone. She's eighteen and has been there since she was four. Her mother's fully involved with the *commune*. It's likely she'd come for Annie if their leader tells her, but not on her own."

"What about her father? He in the picture at all?"

"Nope. Me and Venus are tryin' to see if we can locate him, but Annie's mother won't talk to us."

"Like that'll stop your woman." I couldn't help but grin. Venus could be insistent. Until she got fed up being insistent. Then she did what she deemed the path of least resistance, no matter who she had to run through. Considering she'd been trained as an assassin, she could generally run through anyone if she needed to.

Piston chuckled. "Not at fuckin' all."

As he spoke, the swinging door to the back opened and Annie emerged, tying an apron around her tiny waist. She gave me a small smile before moving to a customer who'd just sat down.

I loved the way she moved around. There was a quiet grace that seemed to wrap her in a cloak. She'd struck me as clumsy at the bikini contest, but that must have been due to an unfamiliar environment because Annie was efficient and deft in her movements. Kind of like a dancer.

"Yep. I can see you're the right one." There was amusement in Piston's voice that was gonna get him a beat down.

"What's that mean?" I barked out the question sharper than I intended, but instead of being intimidated or, God forbid, even more amused, Piston met my gaze steadily with only a raised eyebrow.

"It means, if you tell me you're not interested in that girl, I'll go fuck myself."

"Fuck you, Piston," I hissed. "Even I'm not that much of a dick. She ain't ready for a man like me. Probably never will be and I ain't the settlin' down type. Lost that desire a long fuckin' time ago," I muttered.

"You might be surprised. She's not had an easy time of it, but she's resilient. She's learning Spanish from Elena. Venus has been teaching her Russian. Also, I talked to Chief the other day. He helped us get her out. Took a likin' to that girl."

That surprised me. "Chief? I mean, the guy's pretty amiable and never refuses to help when he's needed, but doesn't he pretty much keep to himself?"

"Yep. But he's been coming to see Annie. To watch out for her. I think he comes here to talk to her when the diner isn't busy." He leaned back in the booth, one leg stretched out away from the table and one arm laid over the back of the booth. "He's teaching her his language. Says she's a fast learner."

"Why me? You must know at least a dozen guys who'd be good for her. I'm way too fuckin' old for her."

"Yep. I could think of at least eight off the top of my head. Unfortunately for you, Venus thinks you're the one she needs." When I opened my mouth to question why, Piston held up his hand to wave me off. "I have no idea why, so don't ask. I just do what she tells me to do. Go where she tells me to go."

"You do hear how pathetic you sound, right?"

"Fuck you too." He grinned just as Annie stepped up to our table, her little order pad in hand.

"Hi, Piston." She gave the older man a warm, genuine smile. "Is Venus coming?"

"Not today, sweetheart. But she said to give you her love."

That seemed to please Annie more than it should have. Her smile got impossibly wider and she looked so happy it was almost painful. "Tell her thank you. And she has my love too. I can never thank you guys enough." She ducked her head, tucking a long, silky-looking lock behind her ear.

"Honey, you never have to thank us. Though if you really wanted to do something for us, I have a suggestion."

"Anything, Piston." She actually looked excited.

"You see this guy?" When her gaze flitted to mine with an uncertain look, Piston continued, "He's in charge of security for our club."

"Grim Road. Right?"

"That's right. I think you met him earlier today?"

"Yes." She gave me a shy smile. "Dominic."

"Annie and I are old friends now," I said, pretending we hadn't just been talking about her. "Piston tells me you're learning a few different languages."

"Oh, yes!" Sweet God, the girl actually bounced on her toes in excitement. There was this strange combination of child and woman about her. Like everything was brand-new and fun, and she was eager to partake. "I'm learning Spanish from Elena, Russian from Venus, and Chief is teaching me Navajo. That one's hard, but so much fun! Chief said I'm picking it up pretty well since I've only been learning a couple of weeks."

"Look, Annie," Piston continued. "I haven't told Dom everything. But, given your situation, me and Venus would feel better if you went to stay at the Grim Road compound instead of at the motel. Marge has done a fantastic job since she bought it, but you're still alone, even with all the extra security she had installed. Would you be willing to go back with Dom? He's got an extra bedroom in his home inside the compound."

She gave me a hesitant look before answering Piston. "Do you really think it's necessary? I don't want to be more of a bother."

"Necessary? Probably not. I'd just rather be safe than sorry. Give Crush and Byte time to look into that camp and make sure they don't decide to come after you."

"I don't think they will," she whispered. She'd grown pale as Piston talked. I'd noticed it and was pretty sure Piston noticed it too. "Not after what I did."

Piston raised a hand. "Honey, anything you did was deserved by whomever you did it to. What do you say? It will make me worry less."

I raised an eyebrow at Piston, who might as well have said, "Take pity on an old man, will you?" Yeah. I couldn't wait to tell Venus about this.

"You promise you have room, Dom? I don't want to take up space you need or be in your way."

"Just me in a two-bed, two-bath house. We can see as little or as much of each other as we like and have as much privacy as each of us needs. You'd be doing me a favor, actually. I've got a dog and a cat. They both like being inside, but I'm not leaving them in the house when I'm not there. If I get tied up and can't get home, I don't want 'em stuck in there. If you stay there, you can let them in and out as they want."

Annie's eyes got wide and round, her mouth forming an "O" of surprise. "You have a cat?"

"And a dog."

"Is it a big dog or a little dog?"

I had to fight a grin. This girl was living life and enjoying the moment. "Medium-size dog. Squirrel dog. She hates the cat."

"And they're both in the house at the same time?"

"Oh yeah. Cat's too smart for the dog. She waits until Peaches is asleep, then curls up on top of him."

That got a giggle out of Annie. "If you're sure."

"I'm sure, honey. We can get your things after your shift and I'll take you home."

Annie flashed a big smile, then readied her pen to take our order. I had the sinking feeling I'd just sealed my own fate. I'd never been attracted to young and innocent, but how could a man resist this woman? I certainly couldn't. I mean, I was *gonna* resist. At least, on a physical level I was gonna resist. I foresaw a lot of sleepless nights and cold showers in my future. And I didn't see me going far from my new charge. My only prayer was that Annie was as innocent as she appeared. It might be the only thing that kept me from throwing caution -- and my self-respect -- to the wind and making her mine. Age difference be damned.

Yeah. I was so fucking fucked.

Chapter Five

Annie

I felt like I was making one stupid decision after another... except maybe I wasn't? Should I trust all these people I didn't know right after leaving a hellish situation surrounded by people I *did* know and still hadn't been able to trust? Probably not. And, honestly, the main reason I had trusted any of them in the first place was because of Venus. Piston came later, but my trust was with the scary woman who dressed in bright pink and rode a motorcycle to match. He'd told me she intended to ditch all the pink, but she'd had to put a club girl in the hospital when she'd come on to Piston thinking he was with someone other than Venus. Apparently, she looked vastly different without the pink.

Speaking of which, I now understood the difference between a bicycle and a bike. Sure, I'd seen Venus on hers, but I hadn't ridden with her. Now, I sat behind Dominic as he rolled down the road with the wind in our hair. Well, his hair because someone had shoved a helmet on my head and I'd been a little top heavy. I also might have squealed and nearly toppled over the back. Only a slight exaggeration since Dom had tugged one of my arms around his waist and still had hold of my wrist when he took off. After that, I had a blast.

As we rolled through some very thick woodlands, I couldn't help the surge of anxiety as reality hit me squarely in the face. Seriously. It was a bough from some kind of evergreen too close to the road and I hadn't been paying attention. Thank God the visor had been partially down or I might have put an eye out.

The most pressing question I had for myself was really very simple. Had I just hitched a ride back into hell? Since Venus had brought me into the real world, I'd heard a phrase a couple of times that I was only now truly understanding. *Too stupid to live*. Yep. I got it now.

But then I thought about Dominic. He hadn't really given me any reason not to trust him. In fact, hadn't I been thinking of him as my hero? There was something in the way he spoke, a sort of gentleness hidden beneath that gruff exterior and the heavy responsibility he carried on his shoulders. He was a protector at heart, which made me feel safer, despite the whirlwind of doubts swirling inside me. It was stupid, but I kind of liked it when he called me girl. Mostly because when he did it now, he winked at me and it made me feel warm inside. Not icky and scared.

We pulled into the Grim Road compound, and it was nothing like what I'd expected. Instead of the ominous biker gang hideout I had pictured, it was more like a small, self-contained village. There were neat houses lined up with small gardens. A couple of children played in the area around a larger building, and people waved as Dominic drove past. It seemed normal, peaceful even. Kind of like the camp had looked from the outside. I pushed that thought hastily away. If I went down that rabbit hole, I'd never find my way out.

There were several bikes parked in front of the main building and raucous laughter and music coming from inside. A woman squealed and stumbled outside, followed by a big guy with a full beard. He wrapped his arms around her middle and picked her up. She let out another squeal before dissolving into laughter. He growled something, turning her in his arms and fusing his mouth to hers. She wrapped her limbs around him, kissing him back and the big guy stomped away from the building and into the shadows.

"Oh, wow," I breathed in a sharp breath.

Dom's deep chuckle vibrated through his chest. He patted my hand as he got off the bike before helping me off. He kept hold of my hand and led the way to a path that led deeper into their compound. I looked over my shoulder and saw a couple of guys closing a chain-link gate with foliage and some kind of camouflage drape to obscure the fence if someone was looking at it from a distance.

There were several houses and neatly kept paths and one small road going deeper into their territory. Some had bright flowers in front of them or in planters on the porch. Others were decorated for the upcoming New Year's Eve party. And some were nearly as Spartan as the huts we lived in at the camp. These houses, though, looked sturdy and not leaky. The open areas mostly had a canopy of the same stuff covering the gate. It made paths through the small village that, even now, children ran through like they might a maze, giggling and chasing each other in fun. I smiled as I watched a group of two girls and a young teenaged boy ducking in and out of the canopies. They were so carefree. Not like the camp I grew up in. It wasn't much, but it was enough to fully shove back the memories threatening to crack through that locked and sealed door in my head.

Dominic led me to his house, a modest, well-kept single-story with a front porch that housed a couple of rocking chairs. Nothing like what I'd live in at the camp. As we entered, a large brown dog came bounding toward us, followed by a sleek black cat that regarded me with curious green eyes.

"You two." Dominic scowled at the pair. The dog whined, ducking his head and moving closer to me while the cat just gave the dog a disdainful look. "What have I told you about being on the porch? You're not allowed. You get hair and muddy footprints everywhere." He sounded appropriately angry, but neither animal scurried from him. Instead, the dog lay down right on top of my feet and looked up at me with a pitiful gaze. The cat licked a paw unconcernedly.

I bent down to pet the dog and he flopped over, his tail wagging between his legs and his paws spread wide. Obviously he wanted a belly rub. Who was I not to oblige?

The dog whined happily, his eyes sliding shut in bliss. The cat sauntered over to me and put her paw on top of the hand rubbing the dog's tummy. She looked up at me and meowed.

"Jealous?" I have no idea why I was talking to the cat. If I'd done it at the camp, I'd have been punished. We weren't allowed to have pets, let alone talk to them. Animals were for work or food. Not for affection.

The cat looked up at me and meowed again.

"Not cool, Peaches." Dominic pointed at the dog, indicating he was talking to him. And I knew it was a him despite the feminine-sounding name. "Not fucking cool."

I swear, the mutt grinned up at Dominic. The lolling tongue wasn't so much the dog breathing as it was him genuinely sticking his tongue out at the big, gruff man. That's how smug he looked.

"He's so sweet. Don't be mean to him." I decided to test the waters. See just exactly what I'd stepped into. Immediately the dog whined and looked pitiful again.

"He's the one bein' mean to me. Makin' you think I'm mean to the bastard." On cue, the dog let out a small, sharp yelp, as if remembering a pain. "See? I'm not a monster. I don't kick puppies." The cat reared up on her back legs, putting both her paws on my knee where I was squatted down, clearly wanting my attention again.

"And you, you little shit." Dom pointed at the cat. "I never said I didn't kick cats. Only dogs."

The cat hissed casually over her shoulder before hopping up to stand on my knee. I had to use both hands to keep her from falling which was obviously what the ball of black, silky fur had planned all along.

I stood, cat in my arms, and regarded the big man. There was a glint of humor in his eyes. Obviously, he wasn't as irritated as he sounded. In fact, I'd say he very much loved these animals. When the dog jumped up from where he was still on his back begging for tummy rubs, he went straight to Dom, tail wagging rapidly and leaned against his leg. Dom ruffled the dog's ears, then the creature moved back to me.

Dom opened the door and the dog immediately bounded inside. The cat, still cradled in my arms, seemed to decide it was her turn for exploration and leaped gracefully from my hold to follow the dog into the house. I hesitated at the threshold, watching Dominic as he moved about, flipping on lights.

"Come on in. Don't be shy. This is your home for the foreseeable future so you need to be comfortable."

His words were unexpected, warming yet also causing a flutter of nerves in my stomach. Home. That was a concept so foreign to me yet so desperately desired. On a small table in the corner of the room some framed pictures were displayed, a mix of family photos and candid shots of people laughing, riding motorcycles, a few of them with Dominic right at the heart. He didn't really seem like the sentimental type so this surprised me. Then again, I'd known him all of two or three hours.

Dominic caught me looking at one photo in particular. It was a younger version of him without the beard, his arm around a woman with a vivacious smile. "That's Tina," he said softly, following my gaze and pointing to the picture in question.

"She's beautiful." A knot formed in the pit of my stomach. This woman was special to him, though it was the only picture on the display with her in it. Next to the photo of him and Tina was another woman who looked remarkably like Tina, but had Dominic's eyes.

"She was." There was sadness in his voice. Regret?

"What happened?" Immediately, Dominic stiffened, then stepped away from me, and I knew I'd asked the wrong question.

"Fear and misunderstanding. I was too young back then. Neither of us really knew what love was, and I had a dangerous job. She's gone, but I have my daughter now. That's the only part that matters."

My heart ached for Dominic. I could feel how much he was hurting. "I'm so sorry. I didn't mean to pry."

He took a breath, then his gaze softened when he looked at me once more. "You're not. I haven't talked about Tina to anyone other than my daughter. We've only recently been reunited." He reached out a hand for me. "Come on. I'll show you to your room."

Taking his offered hand, I followed him down a short hallway. The hallway opened into a cozy living area with a large window overlooking the backyard where the afternoon sunlight streamed in, dancing on the wooden floor. Though the place was pretty sparse, it had some rugs on the floor and a big, inviting fireplace. Dominic led me past this room to another door which was slightly ajar.

"This space is all yours," he said, pushing the door open fully. Inside, the room was simple yet welcoming, painted in soft blues with a comfortable-looking bed covered in a quilt that looked handmade, and good work by the look of it. A small desk sat beneath a window that offered a view of the tall trees bordering the property, and a love seat sat along the opposite wall.

"It's beautiful," I murmured, more to myself than to Dominic.

He smiled briefly, rubbing the back of his neck awkwardly. "Glad you like it. You can change anything you want. Just let me or one of the girls know and we'll make it happen."

"No need to change anything." I smiled up at him, though I felt the distance between us now. "It's perfect. I'm really sorry. I shouldn't have asked about something not my business."

"It's human nature to be curious. If I'd minded you asking, I wouldn't have left the pictures out where you could see them."

"But you didn't know I was coming."

"No," he conceded. "But my daughter would have been happy to remove them for me. Suffice it to say I've had to come to terms with the past I missed out on. At least, I missed being part of it. Tina made sure I got pictures of Calista as often as she could send them."

"Calista is your daughter?"

"Yes. She came to me when her stepfather tried

to sell her to pay off some debts." Dom looked me directly in the eyes and held my gaze with his steely one. For the first time, I began to truly see how dangerous this man really was. "We protect our own, Annie. I don't know what you went through or what Venus pulled you out of, but you're safe here."

I swallowed, unsure how to proceed. "There's something I need to know. I mean, it's not like I've got much of a choice, but I'd just like to know going forward how things work."

"What's your question?"

"Why are you helping me? What do you expect to get from me?"

He gave me a startled look. "Girl, I don't want to get anything from you."

"I don't have any money, but you're welcome to my next paycheck if you want it."

"Jesus," he snarled at me. Then, the oddest thing happened. Dominic moved the distance separating us and wrapped his arms around me, pulling me close to his body and holding me tightly.

I was stunned. What was he doing? I stiffened, intending to push him away, but, after the initial confusion, I registered the warmth of his body seeping through my skin to warm something inside me I hadn't known existed.

I sucked in a breath. Then let it out. When I did, I relaxed into his embrace. It was instinctual and felt more right than anything I'd ever felt in my life. It was like, after a lifetime of lies, I'd finally found the truth. And the truth was, no matter how stupid it might seem or how unrealistic the chances were, I never wanted to leave Dominic's arms.

Chapter Six

Dominic

Shit.

Fuck.

Fuck!

What the fuck was I doing? But, God-fucking-damnit, the second my arms were around Annie, they locked and there was no way I could let go, even if I wanted to. I didn't want to. This woman belonged right where she was. In my arms. And, by God, that was where she was gonna stay.

She relaxed in my hold, inhaling a breath, then letting it out with a contented sigh. I thought she might push away or try to get free, but she actually curled her little hands into my shirt and clung to me. Also, I thought she might be sniffing my chest.

"Mmmm…" Annie moaned, her hot breath heating the skin beneath my T-shirt. She turned her head and inhaled again, this time not even trying to hide what she was doing. She buried her nose against my chest and moaned again. This time with feeling.

"Christ," I bit out, my arms tightening around her without my consent even more. "You can't make noises like that, girl."

My words had the effect of throwing a glass of water in her face. Annie jerked, then looked up at me in shock. Her face blossomed with two spots of color on her cheeks, then a red flush crept from her neck to the roots of her hair. Sweat sparkled on her upper lip.

She stumbled backward and would have fallen on her ass, but I lunged for her without thinking. Again, she was plastered against me, but instead of that glorious desire on her face, now there was wariness and a hit of fear. We stared at each other. I knew I needed to make sure she had her balance, then let her go, but I couldn't. I thought I might be able to let her go if she pushed away again, but the jury was still out on that.

"I-I…" She cleared her throat. Her hands were on my shoulders, and she alternated between curling her fingers into my muscles and relaxing her grip so it ended up feeling like she was kneading like a kitten.

The urge to grin was strong, but I didn't feel much like smiling. I felt the need to wrap her up again and make it clear to her she was never to push away from me again. I needed her close. Insane. I was going insane. It was the only explanation for these feelings swirling inside me. I let her go once I was certain she had her balance, but it was fucking hard. "It's all right, honey. Come on. Let's sit on the love seat and talk. Want something to drink?"

She nodded her head a couple times. "Water." Her voice was rough. She was obviously overloaded and I wasn't sure how off balance I could push her. The last thing I wanted was for her to feel like she didn't have choices.

I nodded to the love seat. "Go. Sit. I'll be right there." She didn't answer out loud, but nodded and did as I told her.

I came back with a bottle of water for her and a beer for me. She took the bottle with a small smile. Not surprisingly, she sat in one corner as far away from me as she could get. She'd snagged one of the pillows Calista had brought to make the room seem more welcoming. Now that I thought about it, there had been pillows and shit in the living room too. What the fuck did my place need to be welcoming for? I hated people in my space. Except I was afraid I would hate it if Annie *wasn't* in my space.

"I'm sorry. I know I'm a freak. I don't act right in front of people."

That was odd. "Not sure I understand, honey." I sat on the opposite end of the love seat, but I reached out to her, holding my hand palm up to see if she'd take it. Surprisingly, she did. She looked at it indecisively for several seconds, but with a look of longing so profound it gave me a visceral response. My chest tightened and there was a lump in my throat for this girl. She'd obviously been through something. It sounded like she'd been part of a gang or something. Maybe even a cult. Somehow, I needed to convince her I was worthy of her trust. That I would protect her and never betray her in any way.

"You know, I'm sorry about earlier." When I gave her a confused look she added, "Asking about the woman in the picture. Tina."

"Nothin' to be sorry about. I never thought of anyone asking. Which was stupid. You see a younger me with a woman and you're genuinely curious."

"I can make it up to you by telling you what happened. It's only right you know anyway since you opened your home to me."

"Only if you want to, honey. Ain't gonna lie and say I'm not curious, but only to know how likely it is someone's lookin' for you. My job in this club is to keep everyone safe. The more information I have, the easier it is to do that job." That was strictly the truth, but the fact was, I wanted to know what happened so I knew exactly who I had to kill to punish whoever had hurt Annie.

She nodded. "That makes sense."

"We've got all night, Annie. Talk about anything you want."

"Well, when I met Venus, I was in a camp with

my mother."

"I see. Did you always live there?"

"Since I was four. It was our home. I don't really remember anything in my life before we moved there, at least, not more than flashes of playing on a playground with other kids or something. When Venus helped me out, she called the place a cult. I've read up on cults in the last couple of weeks. It seems she was right."

"Sounds about what I was thinking. What kind of cult?" It was very hard to keep my voice neutral. If she didn't remember living anywhere else, then Annie truly was in culture shock. It also explained her issues with time and social awkwardness.

"It's called Grace of the Divine. Our leader is supposed to be the voice of God, but even being raised there, I had my doubts. I don't think I was a very good cult member."

"Honey, trust me when I say that's a very good thing."

She eked out a small smile. "Thank goodness, because I thought I was going crazy."

"Most cults have oppressive rules. They're designed to keep you too busy to think and to keep you powerless. If you didn't want a better life, you wouldn't be human. Everyone questions things that make us suffer. You were right to have doubts."

"No one there thought so. At least, not many. And those of us who questioned them were kept strictly isolated. They called it reconditioning, but what it was really was punishment until you came around to their way of thinking." She gripped my hand, adding the other one to it and nervously squeezing.

She continued. "When a girl turned sixteen, they were supposed to be married off to one of the men in the church family. No one wanted me because I was too spirited. That's how they put it. I was too much work to keep in line. So they sent me for reconditioning. The process usually lasts less than a couple months. Not even that long most of the time. When the church elders are finished with the women they recondition, they come out docile and compliant."

"How long'd you stay?"

She winced. "Um, well, a couple of years?"

I raised my eyebrows. "A couple of *years*?"

"Yeah. I'm kind of stubborn." She said that last very softly, as if ashamed to admit it, but also owning it proudly.

"Ain't we all, girl." I tried for a chuckle, but it sounded strained even to myself. This woman... She was breaking my fucking heart. "Is that when Venus found you?"

"Yes. I was making a break for it. I'd gotten out of the wooden box they had me in, but I was so weak from lack of food and water I couldn't scale the fence. I was so frustrated and close to despair that I'd come so far only to be stopped by my own body. That's when Venus found me."

The girl dropped that like it was nothing. She'd managed to get out of the wooden box they'd put her in. Fucking Christ!

"She was in a pink car, sitting on the side of the road. The second I approached the fence, she hurried toward me. I hadn't been able to get more than one step above the ground before my strength gave out. Venus cut a hole in the fence and helped me out just before one of the brothers grabbed me.

"He followed us through the fence, but Venus snapped his neck like she did that kind of thing every day."

"You'd probably be surprised at how accurate that assessment is, but please, continue."

She grinned. "Yeah. She told me she was a trained assassin. I had to ask her what it meant. It's a little terrifying, but Venus isn't a bad person. If she was, she wouldn't have helped me. Not many of the family ever leave the compound, but apparently one of them caught her attention with something he said or did, and she went to investigate. That's when she learned about me. She was trying to work out how to break me out when I broke myself out."

"Now, that sounds exactly like Venus. What pushed you to make the move when you did? I mean, besides the obvious living conditions."

"The Divine One told me he was tired of waiting for me to be reconditioned. He said he was going to use more extreme measures to bring me to heel. He was taking me as his next wife. And he was going to do the ceremony in front of the whole church."

"I'm not even going to ask what that entails because I'm pretty sure I know. Tell me you escaped before he went through with that ritual."

"I did. Thanks to Venus."

I wasn't sure she was doing it on purpose so much as it was a nervous habit, but Annie stroked and explored my hand absently while she relayed her experience to me. Almost like touching me was giving her some kind of comfort. Well, if that were the case, she could do whatever she needed because it sounded like this woman had been through a lot. The fact she could be around a man at all was surprising, let alone be able to touch one.

Before I could think too much about what to say to her next, I spoke. "I met Tina when I was a lot younger. My job meant I was in and out of her life more than a partner should be, because of that and other things, we never made our relationship permanent. In fact, we were only together a couple months before I left her. She knew why. My job, even when I first started in the military, was always very high risk. More than normal because of the type of work I did for the military and the CIA. I didn't want to leave her widowed the first time I left and that was a very real possibility. She didn't tell me she was pregnant when I explained to her why I had to leave, but I'm pretty sure she was. It was maybe eighteen months when she sent me the first baby picture with a letter explaining everything in detail." I couldn't help the smile tugging at my lips as I remembered the pictures and, sometimes, letters that followed. "She would write to me about milestones Calista passed, and describe to me everything she could remember as clearly and distinctly as she could. She understood why I stayed away, but wanted me to be part of Calista's life the only way she could. It wasn't until me and Calista talked about Tina after Calista came here that I realized how much I'd truly loved Tina. And I'd only known her for two months."

"So she was your one true love." Annie smiled and sniffed as she stood. "That's a really sad, beautiful story, Dominic."

"Just Dom, baby. It's my road name and what everyone calls me."

"Dom. Got it." She shifted in her seat, toeing at the rug beneath the love seat a little before catching herself and sitting perfectly still for several seconds. "If you don't mind, I'd like to take a proper shower. We didn't have them at the camp, but it's something I've grown to depend on. I like feeling clean. Also, I love shampoo that I didn't have to make myself. And conditioner. It makes the tangles not as bad."

I had the crazy urge to laugh, but simply nodded as solemnly as I could manage. "I could see how those would be things you'd get used to pretty fast."

"I especially love the hot water part of the shower."

There was no way to contain the chuckle that time. "Yeah, baby. I like that part too. A cold shower is not on my list of favorite things. Not sure I know anyone who particularly likes them."

"Also, you should know that if I ramble or say or do the wrong thing sometimes, I'm not trying to make you look bad for associating with the weird girl, or to look deliberately stupid. Piston says I don't understand social cues. I'm not really sure what that means, but if it's a way of saying I sometimes make things really awkward or uncomfortable, he's not wrong." She gave me a pleading look. "Please be patient with me? Don't kick me out or anything." God, she sounded so fucking vulnerable. Like she fully expected I'd kick her out if she did or said the wrong thing. I think this was the moment I decided I was gonna kill someone. The only question was who and how many.

"Ain't ever gonna kick you out, girl." Emotion threatened to close my throat, making my words gruff and tight. My feelings were all over the fucking place. Probably a combination of telling this young woman about Tina and my own struggle to come to terms with how I felt about Tina. And the way my heart was trying to feel about Annie. And no. I didn't *want* to feel anything other than possibly sympathy or the protectiveness I feel with all the women in the compound. This whole thing where I threw a bikini contest just to find out her first and last name wasn't something I was ready to touch yet. Because something inside me had latched on to Annie Warren. I wasn't certain I'd ever figure out how to unweave those invisible threads trying to bind us together. Worse? I wasn't certain I wanted to.

Chapter Seven

Annie

The next month was what I would categorize as the absolute best time of my fucking life! And yes. I was allowed to swear if I wanted! Which should have been far less exciting than it was. They were just words, after all. What was even better? I could walk around the compound on my own. Sure, there were certain places I wasn't allowed to go, but that went for anyone living in the compound who wasn't actually what they called a patched member. All in all, I don't think I'd ever smiled so much in the whole of my life as I did now. Especially the last couple of weeks as I grew comfortable here.

Living at the compound was a whole new world -- one where I could breathe, think, and just be without the oppressive weight of fear pushing down on my shoulders. I hadn't even realized how anxious and fearful I'd been. Mainly because I hadn't really known to feel any differently. Personal interaction outside of church never ended well. Here, people greeted me by name, asked how I was doing, and actually listened to my responses. It was surreal, like I'd stumbled into some sort of utopian bubble in a world that had shown me little kindness before.

Byte, one of the club's intelligence and information officers, introduced me to computers. And, more importantly, video games and television. Mostly video games. Oh, my goodness, *movies*! There was so much I hadn't known about, or had heard but had no frame of reference. Sure, I'd seen an actual television before Dom brought me to Grim Road, but I hadn't sat down and watched a show. I was too busy just trying to survive. It was on the computer Byte had given me that I'd found I could learn any language I wanted to with a program that teaches those languages. It was the most fascinating thing I'd ever experienced. Which is when I found there were things like that about anything I could imagine. If I wanted to learn how to do something, I just "Googled" it. I loved Google, by the way. The Divine One might not know everything, but I was pretty sure Google did.

Dom was often busy, but he always seemed to have time to check on me. Sometimes he brought me books from the town library, knowing how much I loved to read but was too shy to ask for them myself. Other times, it was a cup of coffee with the perfect amount of cream and sugar. I'd made such a fuss about how wonderful it tasted the first time he'd brought me one that he'd made sure we had a coffee maker in the kitchen and everything I needed to make the perfect cup of coffee. Which, I'd discovered, was a fine art. All coffee was not created equal.

One afternoon, while taking a walk and enjoying the sunshine filtering down through the trees, I wandered down to the small, secluded garden. It was tucked away behind one of the less frequented grounds. There, on his hands and knees, Dom tended to a bed of colorful marigolds and sunflowers. All around him were various vegetables or flowers. His large, tattooed hands moved with surprising gentleness as he cared for the plants. I'd come here with him several times and had helped him. While I could grow fruits and vegetables, I found I loved growing flowers.

"You know, when we first met, I would have never guessed you were a gardener," I said, leaning on the fence slightly amused by the sight.

Dom looked up, his face breaking into a wide

grin. "Helps settle my mind. Call it therapy. Lemon does."

"Can I ask you a question?"

He stopped what he was doing and turned his full attention on me. Other than when I'd done something wrong, no one had ever given me their full attention like Dom did every single day. "You can ask me anything, honey." He wiped sweat from his forehead with the back of his hand. Dirt streaked his shirt and his face in places, but he had the most beautiful smile on a man I'd ever seen.

"You talk about Lemon a lot. Everyone here does."

He raised his hands, almost like he thought I was going to attack or something. "Look, Lemon gives as good as she gets. It's kind of a game with some of the guys. See who can get one over on her. No one has yet. And she regularly busts their balls."

"Theirs," I jumped on quickly. "Not you."

"Nope. Because I never give her a reason to. At least, I try really hard not to give her a reason."

"It sounds like you're actually afraid of her."

To my surprise, Dom answered immediately and emphatically. "Absolutely I'm afraid of her. That woman is vicious on a whole other level." He came toward me and leaned on the fence across from me, a smile still tugging at his lips. "Do you know she actually had Falcon's bike painted pink?" Now, the look of horror on his face as he thought about what he obviously saw as some sort of desecration was so comical I couldn't help but giggle. It was embarrassing. "It's not funny." His eyes got wide and he shook his head. "A man's bike is sacred."

"I'm so sorry." I continued to laugh, unable to stop. I seemed to do a lot of that lately. Laughing. With every outburst of merriment, I felt lighter. Freer. "I imagine it was quite horrifying for him."

Dom snorted out a laugh before schooling his features again. "For all of us. I know I have PTSD just thinkin' about it." He shivered as if someone had walked over his grave. It was one of the funniest things I'd ever seen.

The next thing I knew, I was on my ass in the grass laughing until tears streamed down my cheeks and my belly hurt. Dom sat next to me, putting his arm around me. Without thought, I leaned into him. He pulled me close and kissed the top of my head affectionately.

"You're a remarkable woman, Annie. I'm glad I met you."

I looked up at him and smiled. "There's nothing remarkable about me. I can barely even read."

"Right. You forget you're living with me. I see you every single day. You love to read."

I shrugged, tucking a strand of hair behind my ear to give myself a moment to decide what to say. I knew I was blushing furiously. I loved the feel of him next to me. As I looked up at him, I was sure my heart was in my eyes because I had no filters around him.

"Calista and Evelyn have been helping me. I'm getting better, but I'm pretty slow at it."

"Uh-huh. I also happen to know English isn't the only language you're learning to read. Elena says you translated her menu into Spanish on your own."

"It wasn't all correct. And I tried to tell Tito the other day how much I loved the fries he made me and got my words mixed up. I told him it tasted like dung."

Dom barked out a surprised laugh before he was laughing nearly as hard as I had been before. I couldn't help but gaze up at him in wonder. If I looked at him with hero worship, it was because he truly was my hero. Not only when he defended me at the contest, but how he'd helped me adjust to my new life.

"I'd loved to have been there for that, honey." He wiped tears from under his eyes as he continued to chuckle.

"It was embarrassing!" It had been, but Marge had laughed so hard at the indignant look on Tito's face all of us had ended up all smiles and with stitches in our sides from laughing too much. Tito had hugged me and told me how proud he was of me for learning his language so quickly. Even if I slipped up, I was trying to learn to communicate effectively with the people in my life. His praise had made the slipup worth the small embarrassment. And, really, as Marge pointed out, what was there to be embarrassed about? So I'd messed up a word. What harm had it really done? Tito knew I didn't think his food tasted like dung. Spanish wasn't my first language. I'd never been exposed to anything other than English.

"I'm sure it was. But I don't think you remember it that way."

I smiled up at him. How did he already know me so well? We'd only known each other a month but I felt like he *saw* me. I wasn't someone for him to control or to use until he was done with me. Dom saw me for the person I was. I think he enjoyed my company almost as much as I enjoyed his. I also thought he saw me as a daughter or something and I didn't think I liked that thought.

Did I remember the incident between me and Tito as being embarrassing? "No. But I honestly didn't realize it wasn't so bad until just now. Sometimes, you make me rethink my perception of things."

"Good. You're too hard on yourself and I'm

pretty sure that has everything to do with where you were raised and who you were with." He shifted so he was sitting on one hip, resting the wrist of one hand over his bent knee. "Now, it's my turn. Can I ask you a question?"

"You can ask me anything." I have no idea why, but my stomach started fluttering with nerves. But these were different than any other time in my life. Usually any similar feelings I had were associated with dread. What I felt now as Dom looked down at me with too-knowing eyes had nothing to do with dread and everything to do with anticipation.

"How do you feel about me? Staying with me? Me being all up in your personal space?"

I frowned slightly. "I never thought of it as you being in my space. If anything, I've been in yours." Then that familiar dread stabbed through me. "I-I'm sorry. I thought… I t-thought I was supposed to stay in your home." My breath started coming in short gasps and my chest hurt. I tried to push myself to my feet, but Dom held me down.

"Stop, Annie. Remember perception?" When I nodded miserably up at him, Dom pulled me closer, wrapping his other arm around me. "Honey, I don't want you to leave. In fact, if you tried, I might have to lock you in the house and keep you laughing until you begged me for mercy. No. You need to be right where you're at."

"I don't understand what you mean, then. You're not in my personal space."

"No? We spend nearly every evening together. Every time we see each other in the compound during the day we end up spending the rest of the day together. You seem to like my company as much as I like yours."

"I do." I reached out and touched his chest through his T-shirt, picking at the material. I realized then, I did that a lot. Picked at his shirt. It was a habit I had when I was nervous. About *anything*. If Dom was there, I was always within arm's reach. I'd reach for his shirt and bunch my fingers in it. Dom didn't seem to mind he was my anchor.

"Good. Do I frighten you?"

"What? No! Dom, no. I could never be afraid of you."

"Are you absolutely sure, honey? I never want to frighten you. Ever. You understand me?"

I frowned, not sure where he was going with this. "I understand, but you don't scare me. At all." I huffed out a breath. "I mean, you intimidated me when I first met you, but only for a minute. You give off a safe vibe. At least to me." Yeah, I was babbling again. "Sorry. I'm sure that's way more than you wanted to know."

"No, honey. That's exactly what I wanted to know." He reached out and stroked a finger down my cheek. "You remember the day we met?"

"Yeah. Some creepy guy ran his hand up my leg and you made him stop."

He grinned, curling one finger under my chin while he brushed his thumb just under my bottom lip. "Yeah, I did. I also touched you without your permission afterward."

"No, you didn't. You just freed an aggravating strand of hair from my eyelash."

"I still didn't have permission to touch you. So I want to make absolutely certain you know you have a choice in what happens next."

That was confusing. "What happens next?"

"Yeah. I want to kiss you. But I want you to

know you don't have to. You'll still have a home. You'll still have my protection. And you'll always, *always*, have my friendship."

My eyes widened and my belly did another one of those flips. Excitement. Anticipation. Dom wanted to kiss me?

"Kiss me like the man and woman who came out of the clubhouse the evening I first came here?"

For a moment, a look of confusion crossed his face while he thought back. Then he seemed to remember and grinned at me. "Yeah, baby. Maybe not exactly like that, but that's the way I want to kiss you." I opened my mouth to tell him that, no, that might not be the best idea I'd ever had. What came out was far simpler.

"Yes, please."

Chapter Eight

Dominic

No. Nope. I didn't just tell Annie I wanted to kiss her. And she didn't just tell me yes. And I absolutely was *not* leaning close to follow through with that desire to kiss her.

Except I was.

Slowly, so she had time to pull back, I leaned forward until my lips brushed against hers in a silky glide.

Her response was hesitant at first, a feather-light testing of waters. Then, as if the last piece of a puzzle clicked into place, she melted into the kiss with a contented moan that sent a jolt of need straight to my cock. My heart pounded against my ribs like it wanted to break free. This kiss wasn't just a kiss. It felt like a silent promise, a whisper of all the things I'd wanted my entire adult life but hadn't acknowledged.

I slid my hand up to cradle her cheek gently, brushing my thumb over her baby soft skin. Her hands, those nervous little fingers that had picked at my shirt countless times before, now clung to my shoulders, holding her body close to me. This wasn't the hungry kiss of the couple by the clubhouse. This was something… more. It was hope and starvation. Lust and admiration. She hadn't told me everything she'd endured, but I knew she struggled with something in her past. It was there in her nightmares.

The kiss was soft and sweet but also fiercely determined. The thing was, I wasn't sure which emotions were mine and which were hers. Her feelings were transparent, and during the last few weeks, I could tell she was interested in me. Which made me the worst kind of bastard because I wasn't the type of man to settle down. I was too Goddamned old. Annie wasn't, though.

She was vibrant and vivacious and had the biggest heart of anyone I'd ever met. And she was in my arms. Kissing me as I kissed her. And, fuck if she wasn't fucking delicious.

When we finally broke apart, there was a softness in her eyes that hadn't been there before, a look of trust and something soft but vulnerable. We both were breathing hard. Annie looked up at me with a dazed expression filled with something like wonder. She was definitely not opposed to me kissing her. I wasn't opposed to kissing her either.

For a moment, I just admired her lovely face, highlighted by the orange hues of twilight, her cheeks flushed from our closeness. Then I smiled reassuringly down at her. I stroked her cheek with my thumb before brushing my mouth over hers once more, then slowly sat back, moving away from her.

"Wow." She actually looked giddy. Like this was all a grand adventure. "That wasn't like what I always expected at all." There was a nearly dreamlike expression on her face. Her eyes were half closed and she was so relaxed where she was pressed against me. Like a drowsy little kitten.

I narrowed my gaze. "Oh? How's that?"

For the first time since Annie had come under my care, I saw that serene exterior crack. There were flashes of fear from time to time, but mostly in social situations. The other ladies put her at ease by just being themselves. This was different. Her expression blanked, and the color drained away from her face, her lips almost disappearing into her face they got so pale. She broke out in a sweat and I could see the pulse in her neck speed up and knew I'd fucked up but good.

"I-I'm s-sorry." She stood up quickly and fled back down the path.

"Annie! Annie, stop!"

She didn't. Running back toward the house, she seemed to go faster with each step away from me. At least she was headed back to the home we shared. I knew that's where she'd go because it's where she always went. She had expressed no desire to leave the compound for any reason unless I suggested it. Those times, I always went with her and she'd seemed grateful for my presence.

I'd known kissing her would be a mistake. Getting a taste of the delicate woman who had such a remarkable inner strength while still keeping a gentle nature meant the shriveled up part of my soul had been infused with her inner light. I knew there was no way she could keep giving that to me and not fade away to a shadow of herself, but I knew I'd forever crave that warmth and sweetness. I never wanted to hurt her. Especially not with this.

Considering the nature of cults and women, I had no doubt she had experienced some horrific things. She'd even told me some of it. I mean, she'd been trapped inside a box, for Christ's sake! She'd specifically told me that and I'd been so wrapped up in just trying to absorb all she'd been telling me I hadn't stopped to consider what she'd had to go through during those two years she'd been "reconditioned." I now knew the pain she hid was deeper than I'd realized. And I should have thought to fucking check before I up and kissed her.

"Dom!"

Shit. Fuck. Shit. And piss.

Lemon.

I saw her and my daughter, Calista, headed in

my direction with a full head of steam. Calista hung back slightly, frowning but hesitant, but she continued forward. Lemon didn't hesitate. Her fists were clenched and the fine muscles in her arms bunched as if putting the point on her anger. I stuck up my hand in sheepish greeting like a lame-O, but honestly, there was nothing else I could do. I'd fucked up. Me. So whatever she dished out, I'd take with a bowed head, on my knees. Then I'd walk on my knees back to the house and plead, grovel, beg, or even borrow Falcon's fucking pink monstrosity to ride her round, until she took me back.

Wait. We weren't a couple. Right?

Fuck.

"Hey, Lemon." Yep. I just kept getting lamer and lamer.

"What the fuck did you do to Annie, you bastard?" Lemon wasn't slowing down as she approached and I braced myself for impact. Her hand cracked across my face almost before I saw it coming. Girl was getting good at not telegraphing her movements. Rocket would be proud.

"Lemon!" Calista stopped dead in her tracks, covering her mouth with her hands.

"Sour puss…" Rocket was close behind her, though he was trotting to catch up. Probably had seen or heard Lemon and took off after her. He didn't often try to mitigate the damage caused by his vice president -- she was, after all, the vice president -- but he'd protect his wife with a ruthlessness matched only by the other members of Grim who had women of their own.

"Well? What did you do to her?"

"I kissed her."

Again, Lemon's hand shot out and smacked my

face. The other side this time. And yeah, she was equally quick with both hands. I had to remember to compliment her on that. Once she'd calmed down. And no, I wasn't telling her to calm down. I liked my balls where they were.

"Have you talked to her about what she went through before she came here? Do you know she was trapped in a compound, much like this one, with a cult?"

"I do."

Slap!

"And did you discuss all the trauma she endured?"

I groaned. Hadn't I just been thinking the same thing? "I think you know the answer, Lemon."

Slap! Slap! One side of my face. Then the other. No, I didn't even consider protecting myself. I deserved this for being a horny, possessive, stupid-ass motherfucker who didn't use his fucking brain.

Surprisingly, Rocket hovered, but didn't interfere. I knew he would if he even thought I'd fight back, but my president knew me well enough to know I'd stand there and take whatever Lemon gave me, whether I thought I deserved it or not. I didn't hit women, and if I wasn't man enough to take what they dished out -- as long as no guns or knives were involved -- I was in the wrong position within Grim Road.

"Lemon, stop! Please!" Calista looked like she was near tears, but she only put her hand on Lemon's shoulder.

Lemon slapped me one more time before stepping back. She still looked ready to gut me, but the fact her knife was still at her hip and not sticking out the front of my throat meant she didn't believe I'd done something so bad as to warrant killing. If she'd thought I'd deliberately hurt Annie, or forced that kiss on her in any way, I'd already be dead. Because if she hadn't already ended me, Rocket would.

A long silence followed Lemon's outburst. I didn't dare take my attention away from her lest I end up with that knife in my gut when she thought I wasn't paying proper attention to her. Yeah. I wasn't that stupid.

"Now." Lemon stepped back just far enough to be able to look at me comfortably without craning her neck. "Start over. What happened?"

"Start ov-- You didn't let me start to begin with!" I stopped. Took a breath. This was Lemon. She was pushing my buttons. This is what she did. How she operated. Lemon never made sense. You know. Until she did. "Look, Lemon. I was careful with her. I asked every step of the way. I gave her every opportunity to tell me to go fuck myself. Even encouraged it. She was fine until… after."

When I didn't continue, she stepped forward and slapped me again. This time with feeling. She actually used enough force to turn my head with that one. One thing about Lemon, she was smart when she unleashed her temper. By using an open hand, her palm might sting as much as my face, but it did neither of us real harm and she got to make her point.

"You can keep slapping me all you want, Lemon, but what happened is between me and Annie. I will make it right. I think I accidentally triggered something."

"If you triggered *something* --" she made air quotes --"why didn't you fucking stop?"

"It happened afterward."

"Gonna need to know exactly what you said to

her."

"No, Lemon. And you can't bully me into it. Not this time. If Annie wants to tell you she will. Go ask her. But not right now."

"And what happens right now?" She narrowed her eyes at me, daring me to give her the wrong answer.

"I'm going to go home. Annie will be there and I'm going to find out what exactly happened to make her run, and I'm going to fix it."

She slapped me again.

"Christ, Lemon." Rocket gripped her shoulder and pulled her back, wrapping his arms around her from behind. "You gotta learn when to stop, sour puss."

"I know exactly when to stop." She never took her eyes off me. "I'm not sure he's got the message yet."

Rocket met my gaze. "He did."

Lemon shrugged. "We'll see."

Chapter Nine

Annie

I couldn't breathe. My chest was tight and my heart pounded. Sweat coated my body and my clothes stuck to my skin. My ears rang and my vision tunneled. I had to get inside the house. Lock the door. *Hide*!

The second I got inside and shut and locked the door, my stomach rebelled and I vomited before I even realized I was going to vomit. I knew I should clean it up, but I couldn't do anything but sink to the floor where I landed.

"I'm not there. I'm safe. I'm not there." I chanted the mantra I'd started repeating to myself when this happened. I hated feeling like this! It hadn't happened since I'd come to Grim Road and I was pretty sure it was because of Dominic's presence, but, in a way, the absence of this panic the last month had made this event so much harder. It blindsided me. And for no particular reason! Everything had been fine, then the memory of the last time someone had kissed me hit me like a physical blow.

I rested my head on my knees, putting my hands over my ears. I could actually hear the men in the camp in the reconditioning hut berating me. Jeering. The night before I escaped, the Divine One had stripped me bare and groped me. He said he wanted to make sure I was a virgin, but I'd stopped him. He'd promised he was going to do the ritual marriage ceremony in front of the whole church. The thought of submitting to that vile, evil man, of letting him touch me, letting him have sex with me, was bad enough. But to know he was going to do it in front of the whole church to show them how his expert touch had "gentled" me? To show them all he was so powerful he could even bring the camp's most difficult child to heel? It was disgusting and vile. The whole church was just another way of saying everyone in the compound.

He'd done it before. The man had six wives already. I was to be his seventh. Of course, it might not do him much good to take a seventh wife after what I'd done. Just thinking about it made me nauseous again.

I tried to fight my way through the nausea but that wasn't happening. I vomited before I could get my head turned and puked all over myself. This was it. This was the day I lost my mind completely and couldn't find my way out of the waking nightmare threatening to swallow me whole.

I coughed as I tried to suck in a breath of air and choked on my own vomit. My body was completely out of my control. Every instinct inside me was telling me to run like hell and never look back, but I couldn't seem to do anything but sit here in a pathetic heap.

"Sweetheart, you're safe. I swear I'd never hurt you."

I screamed, turning onto my knees so I could stand and run. I wanted to stand, but couldn't seem to get my legs under me. Not to mention the vomit around me made the hardwood floor slick so my uncoordinated efforts only made maneuvering more difficult. So, I crawled, even as I sobbed in fright.

"Annie." The man calling out to me sounded upset. An angry man was never a good thing in my experience. "Annie!" His voice was sharper this time, his tone letting me know he meant business. I sobbed even more, as I scrambled to the corner of the room behind an armchair.

"*Girl!*"

OK, *that* voice I knew. It filled me with a surge of

adrenaline and I stumbled to my feet. Across the room, hands out to his sides as he put one foot in front of the other very slowly, inching my way carefully, was Dom.

"Girl, listen to my voice. You hear me?"

I nodded.

"Gonna need you to tell me you're listening to me."

My breath sawed in and out of my lungs in a ragged wheeze. I nodded again, then remembered what he'd said he wanted. "I-I'm l-listening." This was so hard! I could see Dominic in front of me, but when he stopped speaking, it was like I was seeing the Divine One where Dominic stood instead.

"That's good. Very good. I need you to take a deep breath and hold it. Can you do that? Hold it until I count to three."

I nodded, then took a couple more breaths before taking one deep breath and holding like he said. Dom immediately started counting. When he got to three, I let out my breath in a rush.

"Very good, girl. Do it again."

I did. Then a couple more times. After the fourth time, the pressure in my chest eased a little and I wasn't light-headed anymore. I was trembling where I stood, but I was starting to fight my way out of the panic gripping me. While I concentrated on taking one breath after another, Dom came steadily closer until he stood right in front of me.

"Girl, I need to get you to the bathroom. I'm going to pick you up. I'm only going to help you. You can always tell me to put you down, but I need to get you to the bathroom."

I gave him several small nods and actually reached for him. The second I did, Dom closed the distance separating us and pulled me into his arms. He lifted me and my legs went around his waist, hanging on for dear life.

"That's it, girl. That's it. You're safe and you know I'll keep you that way. Right?"

"Yes." The word came out a strangled cry. Once the tears started, there was no stopping them. I clung to Dom and *sobbed* and *sobbed*. Through my storm of emotions, Dom held me tight. I was vaguely aware of him setting me on the counter, but I just clung tighter, not willing for him to let me go. He didn't even try to make me let go.

I have no idea how long we were like that, or how long I raged, but when I'd finally worn myself out, Dom gently pulled away from me. He didn't let me go, but he cupped my cheek and made me look at him.

"There's my girl. You know I'd never let anyone hurt you, includin' me." When I nodded, he raised an eyebrow. "Words, girl."

"Yes." I tried to smile but wasn't sure I managed it. "You're back to calling me girl."

"You weren't respondin' to your name. And I don't think you mind me callin' you girl as much as you let on." Oh, his grin was wonderful. Had there ever been a more beautiful man than Dominic when he smiled? There was nothing soft about him, but Dom had shown me more tenderness than everyone in my whole life combined.

"I'll never admit to that."

"You don't have to, honey." He tapped his temple. "I know."

That was when I realized I had us both covered in puke. "Oh, God! This is disgusting! I'm so sorry, Dom!"

"Nothin' to be sorry about, sweetheart. Besides,

I've been in the military or an MC since I was eighteen and old enough to prospect. I've been puked on by more than one man and woman durin' that time. I'm sure this won't be the last time it happens either."

"I'm... not sure what to think about most of that statement. It definitely doesn't give you many points on the intelligence scale." Though I was coming back to myself and tried to make light of the situation to ease the tension, my voice still trembled as I spoke.

He barked out a surprised laugh. "You're somethin' else, girl. Don't ever change. Not one single fuckin' thing."

"Even the screwed up way my brain is? I don't even know what happened, Dom. One minute we were kissing, the next I thought my heart was going to explode."

"I said something that triggered you, honey. What was it?"

"Triggered?"

"Yeah. Something sent you into a panic attack. You said our kiss wasn't what you expected. And I asked you why."

Immediately, that sick feeling returned, but not nearly as violently. I was able to breathe through it this time, closing my eyes and concentrating on taking one breath after another.

"It's OK, girl. You're safe. You're safe." Dom's tone wasn't urgent, just matter-of-fact. Like it was obvious to both of us I was safe, he was just reinforcing the thought.

"He... touched me," I whispered. "The Divine One." Dom went completely still. He didn't let me go, but I could tell I'd shocked him. "It's how I got out of the box they put me in."

"It's OK, honey. You're safe." I know he

probably hated repeating himself -- most people did -- but I also knew he was doing his best to give me comfort and reinforce the notion I actually was safe.

"He was disgusting. They held me while he... while..." I swallowed, bunching my hands in Dom's shirt while I tried to hold down the bile. I didn't want to vomit again because if I got sick I'd have to let go of Dom. "But one of the men holding me lost his grip. I took the ceremonial knife no one realized I could reach and I stabbed him. A few times."

"A few times, huh?" He didn't sound angry or shocked. If anything, he sounded amused. It was enough to pierce the veil threatening to surround me again.

"I did, Dom. I stabbed him over and over. He screamed and the men all jumped back instead of trying to subdue me again. It's how I escaped the reconditioning hut and made it to the outskirts of the camp. I ran as hard as I could to a spot in the fence I knew I had the best chance of climbing. I'd been making halfhearted plans to escape before, but it had been two years since I'd been outside the hut alone. It wasn't as easy to get over as I'd thought it would be. But I made it where I intended to go."

"I know you did, girl. You made it to Venus and she brought you to me."

"I don't think I killed him, but I stabbed him in the privates. Maybe now he won't take any more wives."

"Well, I don't know what he's done since you left, but I can promise you, the second I find that bastard, I can guarantee you he'll never take another wife."

I looked up at him, confused. "How can you promise that? No one can predict the future. The

Divine One tried to get everyone to think he could, but he was lying."

"Girl, I can guarantee it because, the second that motherfucker is within arm's reach of me, he's a fuckin' dead man. I will kill him and I will never even pretend to regret it."

There probably should have been some negative reaction to that declaration. I should have been horrified at the thought that Dom would kill someone, especially because I knew he was doing it for me. This man's death would be as much my fault as it would be Dom's. When guilt and fear didn't come immediately, I waited a few seconds. Then a few more. Huh. "I think I'm a bad person, but I won't regret it either."

He smiled down at me. "That's my girl. Now. Let's get you in the shower. Then we'll watch as many episodes of the baking show you like. I won't even bitch and moan about it. What do you say?"

That startled me. "You won't? But you always complain."

"OK, I might complain a little. But only for fun."

"You're a good man, Dominic." His unexpected confession nearly started up the crying again. I'm not sure how I managed to find this man, but I had no desire to ever give him up.

"I'm just a guy takin' care of his girl."

"Your girl?" My heart started racing again. This was an entirely different feeling. I remembered that kiss. Before my mind betrayed me. That kiss was everything. I knew in my heart, that kiss was how it was supposed to be. Not the perverted fumbling of an evil, controlling man.

"Yeah, baby. You're my girl."

"What does that mean?"

"To be honest, I'm not sure." If he'd punched me

in the gut, I don't think it would have hurt as much as those words. I felt them like a physical blow and I stiffened in his arms and gasped. "Stop, girl!" he snapped. "Let me finish. I'm not sure because I just decided I was headed that way. I was resistant when Piston and Venus approached me because you're too young for an old bear like me. You need someone you can relate to. Not someone who'd been in the military longer than you've been alive. So, I'm not sure what it means because, after I left Tina, I never even thought about havin' a woman of my own. But when you ran from me earlier, I knew I never wanted you runnin' from me again. You run *to* me. I'll keep you safe."

"D-don't give m-me this then rip it away from me. I-I couldn't s-stand it." Tears did start again then. There was no stopping them. I was too emotionally raw and battered.

"Never, baby. I don't think there's going to be any way I could let you leave me, and I ain't panickin' the way I should be at the thought of keeping a woman for my own." He looked so adorably confused, I actually smiled. I could breathe again. The band around my chest finally relaxed and the last of my anxiety dissipated.

"There's my girl." He grinned down at me before leaning in to kiss my forehead. "Now. Shower for both of us. Clean clothes. Junk food. Baking show."

I wrinkled my nose. "Yeah. We both smell like puke."

"Will you be OK by yourself? I don't like leaving you but I know you're gonna need time before you're ready for anything heavy, even if it's only me helping you wash. So if you need me here, I promise to keep it light and strictly nonsexual."

My throat got tight. It was funny how a man the

Divine camp would consider evil was a better person than all of that lot put together. I have no idea why I felt this way, but I trusted Dom with anything. Probably more than anyone else. Even Venus.

I smiled up at him. "Yes. Please stay with me. I promise I'm not going to freak out again."

"And if you do, I'll help you through it. You sure this is what you want?"

I nodded. "I'm sure."

Chapter Ten

Annie

It was harder than expected to strip in front of Dom. He didn't stare at me or touch me. Instead, he busied himself turning on the shower and adjusting the water. He glanced at me once, giving a crisp nod to see I'd removed my clothing but his gaze didn't linger, which put me even more at ease. It helped me shake the last lingering anxiety still inside me and I breathed easier. Before I moved to the shower, I brushed my teeth, grateful to get the taste of vomit out of my mouth.

"In you get." He opened the door to the shower and held out a hand for me to take. I glanced down at his hand then back up to his face. Dom didn't say anything, merely raised an eyebrow, his gaze solidly on my face. It was almost like he was challenging me, daring me to take his hand. To touch him. To get in the shower and trust him to take care of me in this.

I took his hand, stepping into the shower. He gave me a moment, making sure I had my balance, then shut the door. I started to protest, but he whipped off his shirt and shoved off his jeans. When he opened the shower door, he was still in his boxers. He was hard but seemed to ignore it. I thought I probably should feel uncomfortable or scared or something other than relief he'd not left. Shouldn't I want him gone? I'd never willingly been naked in front of man in my life! Yet here I was.

God, this man was beautiful! He was nothing like the men in the camp. The only time I'd seen a man naked was when the Divine One came to me that last time. He and his deacons had been readying to play their sadistic games so, naturally, they'd all gotten naked. There was no one who looked like Dom.

Tattoos graced his skin from the waistband of his underwear all over his torso, arms, and neck. He had some on his legs but not as many. His arms were heavily muscled and vein roped. Muscles played across his chest and belly. His thighs were thick and strong, muscles bunching with every shift of his weight.

Dom cleared his throat and I immediately looked up. The smirk on his face should have irritated me. Or embarrassed me because I'd gotten caught -- what did Lemon call it? -- eye fucking him. Instead, there was a sense of loss because now I had to tear my gaze away and carry on a conversation when I just wanted to stare a while longer.

I met his gaze with what I hoped was a blank expression. Like I had no idea what his problem was. "What." The word came out more like a demand rather than an actual question. No way I was admitting to staring at his... uh... yeah. That.

"Like what you see, girl?" Could the man look any more smug?

I shrugged. "Maybe."

"Maybe, huh? I think I warrant more than a maybe."

"If I admit to more than just maybe, can I ask you for one favor?"

"Hmm... I suppose that depends on the favor. I might need more than an admission of where you were looking. I might want you touch where you want to look." His smile was positively wicked.

Instead of dread threatening to pull me under, I got a hit of adrenaline at the thought of actually doing more than touching Dom's arm or shoulder through his clothes. After everything I'd gone through, looking at a man in a sexual manner wasn't something I ever thought I'd want to. And, yeah, the bikini contest misadventure had clued me into that painful fact earlier, but it didn't look like I was going to listen to the rational part of my brain warning me I needed to protect myself. Besides, either I trusted Dom or I didn't. And for all intents and purposes, I was living with the man. Besides, why would I deny myself something I was beginning to think I really, really wanted?

"You drive a hard bargain, but I think I could make that work."

Dom grinned down at me. "You know I'll give you any fuckin' thing you want, girl. Name it and it's yours."

"When you have him, I want to be the one to kill the Divine One."

* * *

Dom

"What?" No way I'd heard her right.

"I want to be the one to kill the Divine One. I mean, if you were really serious about killing him."

"Oh, I was serious, honey. Just not sure I want you doin' it."

"Why?" Annie looked so serene she might have been talking about the weather. She was probably in shock after her panic attack. It was still eerie as fuck. Like something out of a horror movie where the sweet, child-like woman is possessed and calmly announces to everyone she's getting ready to kill them all. And I'll be Goddamned if my fucking cock didn't stand up and take notice. So not the fucking time for this. Or the reaction I should have had. "I can do it. I'd have no problem and I wouldn't lose a moment's sleep. It might even help me conquer these stupid waking nightmares."

"I can help you conquer them." Slowly, I reached for the shower gel on the shelf next to us. "You don't need to expose yourself to that kinda shit. There's too much sunshine in you for that." I shook my head, trying to clear the unsettling mix of arousal and concern. "You shouldn't have to stain your hands with that kind of darkness, Annie. Let me handle it."

"But I need to, Dom," she insisted, her voice steadier than it should be. "It's something I have to do. I want to make him hurt like he hurt me." Her expression hardened into something I hadn't seen from her before. Oh, she was pissed. It wasn't a hot, explosive anger, something that would burn out quickly. No. There was an ice-cold rage burning in her eyes. Calm. Calculating. She wasn't going to let this go and I didn't think I was strong enough to stop her. I didn't mean physically strong. If this woman wanted something, by fucking God, I was going to give it to her or burn down the world trying.

I studied her face, searching for any sign of the fear or hesitation I might have missed, but found none. Instead, all I saw was determination burning in her eyes -- a fierce, relentless, cold fire that both impressed and worried me.

"OK," I finally said, though every protective instinct in me screamed against it. "But not alone. I'll be with you and you will obey me to the letter. Without hesitation. This is something I absolutely will not bend on."

A smile broke across her face, lighting up her features in a way that made my heart thump painfully against my ribs. Even though she looked happy, two tears overflowed from her eyes and tracked down her cheeks. How had this woman, so gentle and broken, become the center of my every fucking thought? Her lower lip trembled and it took everything I had not to lean in and kiss her until she was so dazed she couldn't feel anything but contentment. And pleasure.

I could see the pulse at her throat beating madly. Her breathing was rapid too. When she parted her lips and her gaze dropped to my mouth, I nearly gave in to the temptation to kiss her.

Turns out, I didn't have to kiss her. Annie put her hands on my shoulders gingerly, sliding them up to twine her arms around my neck. She pressed her wet, naked body against mine and pulled herself up to find my lips with hers.

Like her touch, her kiss was tentative. She brushed my lips with hers but she didn't seem to know what to do next. I opened my mouth and gave her lips a soft lick.

Annie gasped in a breath, her hold on me tightening. Then she mimicked my movement, her little tongue darting out to lap at my lips.

I let her explore, not hurrying her or taking things any deeper than that simple kiss. It didn't take long for her to get bolder and she met my tongue with hers, even letting it slip inside my mouth in a gentle exploration.

When she finally let herself slide back down my body, she looked equally aroused and frustrated. I smiled down at her and brushed my thumb along her bottom lip. Without thought, I pressed my thumb between her lips. She opened and I slid the digit into her mouth.

"Suck." I gave the command in a low rumble. I could barely get the word out, and the second her lips closed around my thumb and she obeyed my order, my knees nearly buckled. It was an innocent thing that shouldn't have felt that good. But the only thought in my mind at that particular moment was how good it would feel if she replaced my thumb with my cock. So, yeah. I might not act on it, in fact, there was no way I'd ever make that kind of move on her -- maybe not ever unless it was her idea -- but I was still going to hell.

"That's my girl."

She hummed happily, her eyes sliding shut like she was in some kind of trance. Occasionally, she blinked slowly. Her gaze always found mine and she looked at me with such trust it humbled me.

Finally, I removed my thumb from her mouth and picked up the shower gel again and handed it to her. "Wash me."

She shivered, leaning closer to me. I kissed the top of her head and she pulled back. Annie squirted a good amount of the liquid soap into her palm before setting aside the bottle. She rubbed her hands together, then turned her palms over and hovered over my chest, hesitating to actually touch me.

"You've already kissed me, girl. Those pretty tits were mashed against my chest, so it shouldn't be any problem for you to touch me with your hands."

She giggled. "Well, when you put it like that." Annie placed both palms on my chest and slowly rubbed my skin in large circles with both hands. A trail of soapy bubbles was left in her wake as the shower gel foamed as she rubbed.

Her gentle exploration moved to my shoulders and arms. Lips parted, tongue dabbing at her bottom lip hungrily, Annie proceeded to torture me for several minutes. She soaped my chest and the upper part of my abs once more. More than once, I caught her peeking at my cock. More than once, I thought she might have the courage to touch. Perhaps not yet, but she would get there. It would take patience and encouragement, but she'd get there. Probably quicker than I thought.

"Will you wash me?" She tried to look like my answer didn't matter to her, but it was obvious it did. The only question was, did she want me to touch her, or was she doing what she thought I wanted her to do?

"Do you want me to?"

She nibbled at her bottom lip and I nearly groaned. Now wasn't the time. I wasn't some horny teenager. I was forty-eight fucking years old. I thought I was past being this turned on, too jaded to really give a fuck about sex as more than a simple release a few times a week. For some reason, with this girl, there was a primal need inside me to claim her. To make her mine and never let her outta my sight.

When she nodded, I shook my head. "Gonna need you to say so, honey. I absolutely will not do anything you don't want. So, until we establish some kind of relationship between us, you're gonna have to tell me exactly what you want. You will trust me to give you anything you want. Yes?"

She nodded again, then let out a breath and gave me a sheepish grin. "Yes. Sorry. I'm nervous."

"We don't have to go any further, honey. We'll rinse off, get into some comfortable clothes, then veg out on the couch. Besides, we've still got half a season to go on your baking show."

Her smile was so fucking beautiful. Hell, Annie was all fucking beautiful. I must have said the right thing because she relaxed, then picked up the shower gel again and held it out to me.

I took the bottle from her, squeezing a dollop onto my palm. The scent of coconut and lime filled the steamy air between us, mixing with a more subtle fragrance all her own.

Gently, I turned her around and started to lather her back, my fingers running in gentle circles and pressing more firmly into the muscles of her shoulders. She let out a soft sigh, leaning back into my touch as if seeking reassurance from the contact. The tension that had been building, the same one that had tightened every muscle in me as I fought against my desires and instincts, seemed to slowly unwind with each circular motion of my hands. She lay passively against me and it fulfilled something deep inside my cold heart I hadn't realized I'd been missing.

"Feel good?" I murmured, keeping my voice low and steady despite the storm of emotions raging within me.

"Yes. Please don't stop."

"Long as you want, baby. Long as you want."

I turned her again and encouraged her to lean her head back. I wet and washed her hair, soaping the long, silky strands into a thick lather. Then I rinsed it clean. I'd just finished when the water started to cool.

"Let's get outta here. Whadda you say?"

"OK." She had a dreamy smile on her face and she was completely relaxed. I had the feeling I wasn't going to have to watch that crappy baking show after all.

I stepped out of the shower, wrapping a towel around her and setting her on the counter. Then I shed my soggy boxers and wrapped a towel around my middle before picking her up again.

I took her to the couch and placed a pillow on the floor in front of me. "Sit, honey. I'll brush your hair, then we can go to bed."

"Mmm..." My guess was the adrenaline was

leaving her system. After her panic attack, I'd expected she'd crash. The shower had served several purposes. She got used to my touch and knew she could touch me, but the soothing stimulation helped bring her down as gently as I could.

I took my time detangling and brushing her hair. I didn't brush it completely dry, instead, I tied it back and braided the long ponytail. I wanted to give her time to settle and drift. It could make getting her to sleep easier. Hopefully without nightmares. She sometimes had them and I hadn't admitted to her that, when I heard her, I always sat beside her bed and held her hand until she relaxed again. Without fail, she laced her fingers with mind and held on tight. Once she did that, she settled. Tonight would be different though. I was sleeping with her wrapped in my arms.

She moaned slightly when I picked her up, her head tilting to rest against my shoulder as I cradled her against my chest. I carried her to her bedroom and laid her on the bed. She was naked beneath the towel and I didn't want to rifle through her things to find underwear or pajamas. Instead, I hurried to my room and brought back one of my shirts.

Once I had her dressed and in the bed, I crawled in beside her and settled her against my chest. She snuggled against me in her sleep, and a contentment I'd never thought to feel again in my life filled my chest. Had it felt this good with Tina? I couldn't remember.

It had been two decades since I'd held Tina like this. If I'd felt this same connection with Tina, it hadn't registered back then. Maybe it was true that you felt emotions more sharply as you aged because right here, in the spare bedroom of my house with this broken little pixie trying to pretend everything's all right when it clearly wasn't, was making me feel all kinds of emotions I hadn't even known I possessed.

I turned my head and pressed my lips to her forehead and left them there. Her skin felt like silk against my lips. It was just one more connection I needed with her.

Annie slept on peacefully and I held her in my embrace. This is the way it needed to be all the time. And, by God, I was going to make it happen. I was also going to find every man or woman who hurt my girl and make them pay. Then, if they were lucky, they were going to die.

Chapter Eleven

Annie

I was going to kill Dom.

The man hadn't left my side in two solid weeks. I was barely able to go to the bathroom by myself. When I did, he was always nearby, waiting for the door to open. He took me to parties at the main clubhouse, though it was way more sedate than I'd expected. When I'd asked Dom about it, he said the wild parties happened in town at the new clubhouse they'd acquired so they weren't constantly coming and going from their "hidden" compound.

None of that was important. What had me ready to kill the man was how gentle and careful he was being with me. He insisted on going slow and by slow I meant it was starting to feel like we'd be into the middle of the next century before he did more than kiss me. I thought he wanted to have sex with me, but he was holding himself back. And I was tired of waiting.

I was buzzing with a mix of frustration and anticipation. I knew what I wanted, and every inch of my body screamed for it, but Dom was playing by some rule book I hadn't read. After the life I'd just left, being in the Grim Road compound had changed how I dealt with things. I'd always had to be patient and careful. Lemon and Calista especially had shown me that I didn't have to weigh each decision I made. That it was OK to sometimes make the wrong decision. Most importantly, I'd learned I didn't have to be patient all the time. So I was done. It was time to take what I wanted. If I had another panic attack, Dom would help me through it. There wasn't even a question.

Dom was always up early. I hated mornings. Had come to loathe getting up before at least noon. Why? Because there had never in my life been a time when I could stay in bed if I wanted to. I had no idea it was even an option to not be up when the sun first climbed over the horizon. So, he never woke me when he left, but he did leave me a note on his pillow telling me where he'd be when I got up and was ready to go outside and today was no exception. But today, I wasn't coming to him.

At twelve-thirty, I heard him enter the house. I took a breath to calm myself. This was the moment of truth. If he rejected me, there'd be no going back. I'd have to find somewhere else to live because I needed Dominic like I needed to breathe. I'm sure a psychiatrist would have a field day with everything rattling around in my head, but Dom was my choice. If I couldn't have him, I knew I couldn't be around him.

I'd prepared as carefully as I could, showering and shaving everywhere. That had been Lemon's suggestion. No, I do not want to relive the conversation. I'd lotioned my body until my skin was soft and silky. Then I'd draped a thin sheet over my body and settled on my side in the bed facing the door and waited for Dom to come check on me.

"Annie?" he called out to me as he shut the door. "Honey? Where you at?"

This was it. "In the bedroom, Dom."

I heard his heavy footsteps move down the hall toward me. I broke out in a sweat and it felt like my heart was going to pound through my chest. This was a bad idea. So fucking bad...

"Baby, you good?" he spoke as he rounded the corner, his gaze automatically focusing on me the second he could see inside the room. His eyes widened and he came to a sudden stop just inside the doorway. "Annie?" The question was a husky growl. "What the fuck are you doin'?" He sounded like he was musing to himself rather than asking me a question.

His gaze ate me up. Dom clenched and unclenched his fists as if fighting himself to keep from doing something he knew he probably shouldn't.

I raised myself up onto one elbow, letting the sheet slip down just enough to reveal more skin. My breath hitched as I watched his reaction, his eyes darkening with desire yet filled with confusion.

"Dom," I started, my voice a mix of determination and vulnerability, "I'm tired of waiting. I know what I want."

Dom closed the door gently behind him and took a cautious step forward. His jaw clenched as if he was battling internally. "Sweet God, Annie. Are you fuckin' sure?"

My breath caught. This might actually be going to happen. "I've never been more sure of anything in my life. I think I've been waiting for this since before I escaped. But only with you."

He didn't move. I could see the indecision on his face. I could also see desire growing by the second. When he took one slow step forward, Dom scrubbed a palm over his mouth. I watched as he eyed me from where my toes peeked out from under the sheet, to where it was held in place over my breasts by my arm.

"Christ, you're beautiful." He took another step forward. One slow step at a time. When he finally made it to the bed, he sat down carefully, like he was afraid of scaring me and expected me to bolt at any moment. He reached out and brushed a finger down my cheek, then brushed my lip with his thumb. "You can always tell me to stop, honey. I don't care how far it goes, if you want or need to stop, tell me and we stop."

"What if I just need a second? Can we maybe back off but try to continue?"

"Absolutely, honey. You're in control. I'm here for you."

I let the sheet pool around my waist. "This is as far as I got when Lemon told me what to do to get you to fuck me. She said I'd figure it out and if I didn't, you'd take it from here."

That seemed to snap him out of his trance. His gaze found mine and he let out a surprised chuckle. Then he really laughed. The sound was infectious and I found myself smiling. The tension drained out of me when Dom scooted farther onto the bed and rolled halfway on top of me, pinning me underneath him.

His laughter still rumbled within his chest as he hovered over me braced on one forearm, his eyes twinkling with a mix of mirth and raw desire. "Lemon. Of course she had a hand in it. I gotta say, though. She might not have written the best instruction manual, but her advice wasn't half bad," he murmured, his voice deep and soothing. "Though," he continued, "I think we can improvise a little from here. What do you think?"

The anxious knot in my stomach loosened at his words and the tender way he gazed down at me. His large hand, warm and reassuring, slid from my cheek down to my shoulder, and I felt every last bit of tension ebb away. "I think that's a brilliant idea," I managed to say, my voice steady despite the pounding of my heart.

His weight on top of me felt comforting, grounding, and I felt a surge of relief. Here was Dom, not pushing away but pulling me closer to him. It was a new sensation, this mixture of safety and exhilarating danger. I reached up to thread my fingers through his hair, pulling him down for a kiss. His lips met mine with a fiery urgency that belied his earlier hesitation. Not that I minded at all. His desire fueled my own. If I hadn't been sure before, I was definitely sure now. I needed him to show me what sex was supposed to be like. And I wanted to belong to him in every way possible.

The kiss deepened, the feel of his shirt rubbing over my nipples electric. Dom's let his hands roamed over the curve of my waist, up to cup my breast gently as if I were something precious.

I realized as he kissed me so reverently, that from the moment I'd met Dom, he'd *seen* me. Sure, we'd gotten off to a rocky start, but it hadn't been all that bad. He'd irritated me, but he'd also taken care of me. He accepted me just as I was. Annie, who'd never been loved before. The thought alone was enough to make my toes curl with pleasure.

With a murmur of agreement, Dom rolled off me and tugged the sheet away and tossed it over the side of the bed. Then he reached for the hem of his shirt. His chest was smooth and muscular, a temptation I couldn't resist touching as I leaned in to place a kiss over his heart. As he stripped off his shirt, I found myself tracing the lines of ink on his skin.

Once he'd gotten rid of his shirt, he lowered himself on top of me, moving between my legs. I was naked, but Dom still had on his jeans. The scrape of the rough material against my bare pussy was a curious mixture of discomfort and pleasure. It wasn't pain, exactly, but it wasn't comfortable. I was too sensitive, but I absolutely did not want to lose that delicious friction.

"Kiss me," I whispered. "I love it when you kiss me."

He obliged me with a sharp grunt. Unlike every other time we'd kissed, there was an edge of wildness to this. His beard tickled my face as he deepened the kiss. He thrust his tongue inside my mouth and I whimpered in excitement. Gripping his shoulders, I dug my nails into his skin to hang on and hold him close.

Dom pulled away, panting. "You're so fucking beautiful," he growled as if trying to keep it together. His lips trailed down my neck in a line of hot kisses that made me squirm beneath him. Then he leaned back, eyes on fire.

I smiled up at him, unable to speak as Dom positioned himself over me once more. This time he rocked his hips back and forth between my legs as he settled himself where he wanted to be.

"I wasn't expecting to come home to this." His voice came out in a hoarse whisper. "You've had me hard for you for weeks, so when I say this is gonna be quicker than I'd like, know that's not an easy thing for me to admit to." He sounded disgruntled, but I thought he was trying to lighten the mood. "Ain't never wanted a woman the way I want you, and that's also damned hard to admit."

Maybe I should have been offended or felt like I was being compared to countless other women in his life, but it felt oddly satisfying. If that made me shallow and stupid, then I guess he had me pegged because I was taking him at his word.

"I don't mean to ruin the mood, but I need to know if you've ever had sex before. In any way. I absolutely will not hurt you in this. Especially not if it's your first time."

"No. The Divine One tried to have sex with me, but I stabbed him before he could." I stiffened, waiting for the familiar fear to hit me at the mention of the Divine One, but it didn't come.

"Honey? You good?" Dom's expression was calm and controlled.

I smiled up at him. "I've never been better in my life. I thought for a second the mention of his name might bring a rush of revulsion, but this is so different from that experience it simply doesn't apply."

"It'll take a brave woman to be by my side, Annie. Not because you'd ever be in danger, but because you'll have to push back because I will totally take over as much of your life as I can if you let me." He grinned. "You're that brave. Probably more. So I'm going to trust you to know what you can take and what you can't. I'm also going to trust you to tell me when I need to stop."

"How very good of you," I said dryly. "I know how to stop you from doing something I don't like. But I won't have to stop you. I'm betting you'll be able to tell if I like something before I do."

He raised an eyebrow. "You complainin'?"

"Not at all. Now. Are you always so chatty during sex?"

"Brat." Then he kissed me again.

Dom cupped my breast in his big hand. I gasped when my nipple rubbed against his roughened palm. He kneaded and tugged before shifting his position and bending his head to my chest.

I cried out, arching my back to offer my breast to him. He sucked at my nipple gently before opening his mouth and taking more of my breast into his mouth. This had me bucking against him, my clit ached and throbbed and I shivered uncontrollably.

"Dominic! What is this?"

He chuckled and moved his hand to my other breast. He kneaded it like he had the first one only to tug on the nipple with his fingers. All the while he continued to suck my other breast.

I thrashed under Dom. He didn't seem to notice, or if he did he didn't mind. As I moved, I managed to align myself perfectly against him so I got the friction I needed on my clit. The second I did, I tightened my legs around his waist and got all the pressure I wanted exactly where I needed it.

There was no containing the scream of pleasure when that wave crashed over me. All I could do was ride it out wherever it took me. My body seized and pulsed for several seconds. When it finally floated me into tranquil calm, Dom was reaching between us to unfasten his jeans.

"Christ, Annie! You came so fuckin' hard, didn't you."

"C-came?"

"Yeah, baby." He grinned at me, but it looked strained. I knew how he felt. There was still a torrent inside me wanting free. This was insane! "I'm not gonna last long, but I swear I'll make you come again before I do."

I felt him against my entrance, the blunt tip of him pressing into me one shallow thrust at a time. He hadn't much more than gotten the flared head inside me when I felt a pinch. I sucked in a breath.

"That's it. Another deep breath, baby."

I obeyed and Dom flexed his hips, driving his cock inside before retreating, then surging forward again. He did this a couple more times before he could go no farther. Each thrust stretched me, burning but making me long for more of the blinding pleasure of before.

"Dom -- Dominic!" I gasped out as sensations began to build inside me again. This time, the full feeling in my pussy where his cock pulsed angrily added even more to the building tide. I wasn't at all sure I was going to survive this, and I started to panic. Not like before. No. This was my heart's last-ditch effort to not get broke. I'd known this would change our relationship dynamic. My mind knew Dom would never break my heart intentionally, but I saw more than one of the unattached women -- they called them club girls -- look at Dom. If one of them touched him, I couldn't promise I wouldn't do something rash. Because I absolutely would *not* share this man with another woman. The thought of one of them touching him, even if he rebuffed them, made me want to claw someone's eyes out.

"Now, what's that look about?" There was a wildness in his eyes that seemed to mirror my own possessive feelings. He flexed his hips and I arched my back on a groan.

"Dom…"

"Yeah, baby. It's Dom inside you. Me. I'm bare and I'm gonna put my cum inside that sweet little pussy." Thank God we'd already had this talk long before we'd started this. It had been one of the first relationship conversations we'd had after he'd first kissed me. He'd had a procedure done so he couldn't have kids. Said as much as he loved Calista, he hadn't been able to protect her because he hadn't been in her life. He never wanted to take the chance of that happening again.

"O-OK." Not the brightest thing I'd ever said, but I couldn't bring myself to care overly much. All I cared about was the end result. When he made me come again. Because he said I would before he did and I really, *really* wanted to come again.

He hooked his arm under my knee and shoved my leg against my chest. Then he angled his body so he hit just that little bit deeper inside me. On the second thrust, my muscles seized to the point of pain.

The orgasm built inside my body at the place where we were joined and pushed through my belly and chest. My pussy clamped down on him, and his cock pulsed like mad. Dominic bellowed above me and I actually felt his hot seed spilling inside me.

"Annie." He groaned my name as he collapsed on top of me. His breathing was as ragged as mine and we lay there not moving. He was still firmly inside me. "So fuckin' mine…"

Chapter Twelve

Dominic

"And then, I wrapped my arms around both Apple and Lemon and held on tight." Ringo relayed the story of how he'd gotten the keys to his and Calista's house the month before from the two sisters. Piston and Venus listened with equal expressions of amusement to Ringo's retelling of the encounter. His gleeful exuberance amused me to no end. Especially since I knew he wouldn't have the last word in this no matter how embarrassing he tried to make it for the twins. OK, so mostly he wanted to tell on Lemon. Still wasn't going to end well for him.

We were at the new clubhouse in Riviera Beach. The club had a private beach adjacent to the property. Annie needed to get out of the compound and start to live as normal a life as she could considering she was going to be the old lady of Grim Road's sergeant at arms. Which was to say, her life would never be "normal," but the club was pulling together to help her settle in and we were all doing our best to show her how different her life was going to be. Everyone in this club had come together as a family and Annie was part of that family.

"Like, you hugged them or something?" Piston's lips twitched, but he seemed to be doing his best to keep a straight face. Venus just shook her head.

"Yep. Totally did. Thought Lemon was gonna freak the fuck out."

"Apple didn't stab you?" Venus raised one pink eyebrow. She wasn't smiling, but I could see the humor dancing in her eyes. Funny she hadn't asked if it was Lemon.

"Well, I don't think she was actually armed at the

time, but that's not the point." Christ. Ringo was my enforcer and a fucking good enforcer, but sometimes, he was just a dumb fucking shit. Then I glanced down at Annie. She had a smile on her face and was paying rapt attention, eating up every single word Ringo uttered.

"What exactly is point?" Venus crossed her arms over her chest as she leaned casually against a tree.

"The point is Lemon did an icky dance. An actual icky dance. She shook out her hands like she had shit on them and did some fuckin' little shimmy" -- whereupon Ringo demonstrated --"and started whining about Ringo germs."

Piston and Annie cracked up. Ringo looked supremely pleased with himself. Unfortunately for Ringo, Lemon had been approaching and saw the whole "icky dance" thing. She just happened to be on his blind side so Ringo didn't see her. When she smacked him in the back of the head, Ringo flinched and ducked a little, wincing before whipping his head around to see who'd attacked him.

"The fuck, Lemon?" She held up her index and middle fingers, pointed from her eyes to Ringo, then kept on going without a word. Annie was now rolling in the sand laughing her ass off, and Piston was wiping tears from his eyes. Calista was next to Annie in the sand, laughing just as hard as the other two. "Way to throw a guy under the bus, Calista. You're supposed to be on my side, not the hellion's."

"You're my man, and I love you, Ringo, but you will never get the best of Lemon. I'm not sure why you try so hard."

Ringo gave my daughter a disgruntled look. "Your daddy needs to catch up on all the spankings you missed out on as a child."

Calista grinned up at him. "Tell you what, baby. If you're good, I'll let *you* spank me."

"Oh, no you don't," I snapped. "No having kinky sex with my daughter. Which means no kinky sex for you at all since you can't have sex with anyone other than my daughter, Ringo." I thought about that for a second, then decided to add something. "In fact, you can't have sex with my daughter since my daughter is too young to have sex, so no kinky sex at all. Ever." I glared at my enforcer, daring him to try and get out of this one. "You're just shit the fuck outta luck on this one, you bastard."

"Dad, I'm old enough to have sex."

Ringo winked at me and I knew this whole thing had likely been staged for Annie's benefit. Which had most likely been suggested by Calista. The two women were solidly fast friends now. In fact, every single woman in Grim Road had welcomed Annie into the fold. The club girls even stayed away from the catty behavior around her. Which might have been Lemon's doing, but I'd noticed more than one of them sharing a laugh or smile with Annie. One or two had some serious conversations with her. Not of a mean nature, but I knew most of the women here had fled some pretty bad circumstances. While I didn't like digging into anyone's private lives, Crush and Byte fully investigated every single person we'd ever brought into our territory. They'd passed on pertinent information to me about everyone. At least one of the women had come from a cult as well.

"No sex." I pinned Ringo with my fiercest stare.

"Wouldn't think of it, boss." Ringo had a shit-eating grin on his face. Probably because, despite what I was willing to admit, he was about to get laid if the look on Calista's face was any indication.

Christ! My life!

"Where's my little *chica*?"

I turned to see Elena and Tito headed in our direction. Lemon was talking with Tito as she led them to us. When Elena saw Annie, her face lit up and she hurried to my woman. They embraced and began a spirited conversation in Spanish.

"You should be proud of that girl." Tito greeted me with a smile and a warm handshake. "Elena says she's close to fluent in *Español*. She learned quickly."

"Venus says the same," Piston offered as he reached for Tito's hand. "Those ain't the only two languages she's learning either."

I grinned at them. "Nope. Girl's learning the most common ones. Seems to love languages."

"She'll be a good hidden asset."

"Don't plan on usin' her as an asset, Piston."

"Nope. I never planned on usin' Venus either."

"You're not using Venus." I was confused as to where he was going with this.

The bastard clapped me hard on the shoulder and chuckled. "Exactly."

I barked out a laugh. "I'd love to say my woman didn't have that in her, but I'm seeing glimpses of what she's like deep inside. She's a warrior. I just don't ever intend for her to have to be a someone we use. For any reason. I'll fuckin' kill anyone I have to keep her from being an asset."

"You realize you sometimes don't have a choice in the matter. Right?" Tito chuckled, shaking his head. "I never wanted to own a diner. Hated the thought of it."

Piston snorted. "You think I wanted to have to make nice with people? That's what ambassador means. You make nice with people."

"I'm pretty sure there's more to it than that, old man." I felt a smile tugging at my lips.

"Not much. Luckily, Venus handles everything and other than Thorn and El Diablo, the others pretty much live in fear of her. Mama and Pops have encouraged the fear." Piston looked like he couldn't be prouder. "So far it's not been too bad. Right now, you guys are the subject of her focus because of your woman."

"Oh? How's that?"

Piston leveled a look at me. "She's making sure you do things right with her."

"Ah. So Lemon and Calista got her away from me to interrogate her." When Piston grinned, I flipped him off. "You turned my own daughter against me. Some things gotta be sacred, Piston."

"Take it up with Venus." Piston pulled out a joint and lit up. "I'm just here for the pot."

Yeah. This place was one big family. Brothers and little sisters all. I loved it. I think everyone else did too.

The women sat at a stone bench under a huge beach umbrella, talking and sharing a bottle of Crown Royal. It was something Lemon had picked up and fallen in love with. Last time she'd brought it out, Annie had been drunk off her ass. She'd had an amazing time and, surprisingly, hadn't been hung over the next day. Probably because I made her drink a bottle of water for every two shots she did. Overkill? Maybe. But for her first stem-winder, I figured the extra water would not only help her stay hydrated, but fill her up so she didn't drink as much.

"They're here," Piston said, his gaze was lasered on the entrance to the beach. A small group of men approached them with Bear and Spike flanking them with Rattler leading the way while Leather and Rocket brought up the rear.

"Took them long enough."

Piston shrugged. "Chief said they debated on leavin' her be. She did a number on their leader, though. He's the tall son of a bitch in the middle of the group. Not sure how much function he's got left in his dick after she got through with him. Includin' not bein' able to piss standin' up."

"That's my girl." I kept my tone light but I was readying myself for a fight.

I glanced over at the women. Looked like they'd multiplied. All of them surrounded Annie in a protective ring. They were still laughing and talking and seemingly oblivious, but Cecilia and Evelyn glanced at the incoming group more than once. Luke, Evelyn's oldest child, positioned himself in the sand on a beach lounger between the visitors and his mother. That kid was going to be a force to be reckoned with when he grew up.

Rocket hung back while the rest of the group walked up to me. A tall, slender man in the middle stepped closer, moving between the two men in front of him. He was thin but wiry and very aware of his surroundings. I saw the exact moment he spotted Annie, and he hid it well. But I was very good at my job. He carried himself like a man who knew what he was doing and I had no doubt he could hold his own in a fight. Was he the most dangerous man in the area? No. Besides our guys, the man immediately to the left was the one to take down first in this group. He was also the most likely to draw first blood.

Everyone in the group dressed in black jeans and black shirts. Which kind of surprised me because they didn't really fit the classic cult profile.

Rattler brought the guy to us. His entourage followed only a couple of steps behind their leader. The only guy who seemed uncomfortable with the setup was the man I'd identified as the one to watch. Yeah. He knew something was up. He touched the leader's shoulder lightly but said nothing. The other man acknowledged him with a slight tilt of his head.

"I'm here for Annie."

I said nothing. Piston took another draw off his joint.

"I see she's here." He waved his hand in the direction of the women. "While I appreciate you looking after what belongs to me, I'm here to collect her now."

I still said nothing. Piston passed me the joint. I took my own hit and passed it back.

The cult leader raised a hand and signaled to the men in his group to go to Annie. Leather, Spike, and Bear formed a wall between the women and anyone trying to get to them.

"Not your best move." Venus approached from the other side. By now, there was no distracting Annie. She saw the commotion and was trying to head in this direction. Lemon and Apple spoke with her, encouraging her to hang back. Apple tracked the movements of the men in question. She and Deacon had come for an extended visit. It wasn't long before Deacon joined the men standing in front of the women. "You should sit with Rocket. Talk." Venus's voice was lightly accented Russian. She sounded reasonable, but anyone would have to be a fool to think she wasn't ready to kill a motherfucker. "Will be, shall we say, enlightening conversation."

The same guy I'd pegged to watch earlier leaned in and whispered something to his leader. The man smiled at me, apparently assuming I was the one in charge. "Forgive me. I should introduce myself." He had a slightly Asian look but appeared to be more of an ethnic blend. A couple of the men with him were similar. I could tell they were speaking to each other softly. Since I could read lips, I knew they weren't speaking English. "I'm the Divine One, leader of Grace of the Divine. You have one of our family in your midst. In fact, she's my wife. I must insist you return her to me." His accent was slight, but still there. It was definitely some relation to an Asian dialect, but I couldn't place it.

I glanced at Rocket who stood with the other men in Grim between the cult and our women. Lemon approached from behind the men with Annie in tow. Lemon refused to let the younger woman past her but didn't try to keep her away from our visitors as I'd have liked. I saw Annie say something to Lemon and the VP gave her a crisp nod in acknowledgement.

"Ah, my wayward bride." The creep smiled at Annie. She flinched, but held her ground, putting her chin up. "Come then. Tell your new friends goodbye and we'll go home."

Annie found and held my gaze for a moment. I gave her a nod. "I am home." Her voice was clear and strong. I could tell she was nervous, but she was facing her nightmare. I was incredibly proud of her.

"Don't be silly, child. You don't belong here."

"Yes, I do."

The Divine One smiled, then spoke to his guard. "*Dāng wǒmen líkāi shí, bǎ tāmen dōu shā diào.*" The guard nodded and stepped away from the Divine One, to the center of the eleven-man group.

Annie's eyes widened and she found my gaze.

Her breathing quickened, the pulse fluttering at her neck. I narrowed my eyes and tilted my head slightly, not understanding what I'd missed.

"Is there anything I can do or give you to make you give her to me?" He still addressed me but I wasn't saying anything. Something felt off. Maybe I was hypersensitive to Annie's obvious distress or maybe there was something I wasn't seeing.

Annie's gaze darted to Venus. "*Oni sobirayutsya ubit' vsekh*!" she yelled in what I assume was Russian across the gathering. Venus immediately pulled a knife and charged the group…

And that's how the fight started.

Chapter Thirteen
Annie

I wanted in this fight. Rage erupted inside me. Surprisingly, it was Lemon who kept me back. She was backing me and Apple away to relative safety where the other women were. I thought it odd Lemon didn't jump in the fray, but figured she had her reasons. I was glad that yelling to Venus in Russian what they'd whispered to each other in Mandarin threw them off just enough to let Grim Road get a jump on them.

"Where's Elena and Tito?" I thought Elena was close by, but Tito had been with Piston and Dom not long before the Divine One and his deacons arrived. The beach erupted into a cacophony of shouts and sounds of struggle. Dust and sand flew up as bodies collided. Venus was a blur of movement, her knife flashing in the sun as she engaged one of the Divine One's guards. Spike and Bear had teamed up against two other men, their large forms towering over their opponents as they used brute force to subdue them. Dominic wasn't trying to kill his enemy. They wanted these men alive. At least, for now.

Rocket and Leather cut off potential escape and Dominic fought by his president's side. I looked for Lemon. Though Lemon was still urging everyone back down the beach to the clubhouse, I caught her glancing over her shoulder occasionally. Where before she'd been completely focused on getting everyone to safety, now that we were all moving in the direction she wanted, I could tell she wanted to be in the fight with her husband.

Tito hurried Elena to our group before kissing her briefly and heading back to the men. More of the Divine One's men came down an embankment above the beach.

"There are more coming," Elena gasped out, winded from the short run. "From the trees."

Lemon immediately pulled out her phone and tapped out a message. "Reinforcements on the way," she muttered to herself. "Now, Elena, will you please make sure everyone gets back to the clubhouse?"

"You should come too." Elena gripped Lemon's hand, pleading with the younger woman to come with her.

Lemon patted her hand kindly. "You know I have to keep Rocket out of trouble. Besides, my sister will want to get back to help her man and I can't let her go alone."

"I'm coming with you," I said. "This is my fight."

Lemon gave me an assessing look, then nodded. "Fine. But you do what I say. I'm not letting you get hurt just when Dom found you."

By the time we got back to the fight, Grim Road had it mostly under control. The men coming in from the cliffs had tried to retreat but, when they reached the top, there were more men waiting on them. I didn't recognize any of them, but it was clear by their body language, the Divine One's men weren't happy.

"We got a trailer?" Rocket had a phone to his ear talking with someone. "Good. Bring it to the beach. We've got some trash to take out and I'd rather make sure it stays gone." Rocket stuck his phone in his back pocket. "You guys good, Lemon?"

"Yep. Everyone was headed up to the clubhouse when we came to check on you guys." Lemon moved to Rocket's side but didn't touch him. "You finished without me."

"Sorry, babe. Next time." Rocket smiled down at Lemon fondly. It was clear the two loved each other very much. The thing was, I'd seen that same look on Dominic's face when he looked at me.

I sucked in a breath. Yes. I'd definitely seen that look on his face. And it hit me. Maybe this wasn't a dream, or wishful thinking. Maybe I was truly going to get the happy ever after.

Dom finished securing the prisoners. The Divine One was angry as hell. When his gaze landed on me, he tried to lunge, snapping at me.

"Fucking bitch! You would have been my greatest treasure. To think I wasted my time on one so unworthy." He gave me a superior look even though he was the one tied and sitting in the sand on his ass. He still saw me as somehow less than him… because I was a woman who didn't obey.

I'm not really sure what happened next. One second I was standing there contemplating how best to kill the vile, evil little man, the next I was covered in blood and Dom was pulling me off the Divine One, who lay in the sand with blood pooling around him. It looked like someone had stabbed him in the throat a few times. Judging by the blood covering my hands and arms, I was guessing that someone was me.

* * *

Dom

I saw it happening and wasn't fast enough to prevent it. Annie snatched the knife from Lemon's hip and threw herself at the man she'd named as her tormentor. After that, there wasn't really much point in stopping her. Luckily, there was no way to see this stretch of beach from the road. You had to climb over the cliff-like embankment and around the base of the rocks to be able to see what was going on where we were. It was why we chose this place -- our private beach -- to meet with this fucking cult when Byte found them three days before the Divine finally approached us. We knew we were going to kill them, but no one had thought it would be Annie who'd do it.

The scream she let loose was bone chilling. I like to think the last thing that went through that bastard's head was to know the devil was coming for him and had sent a banshee to send him to hell.

The other cult members blanched and whimpered. A couple tried to crawl away but the men surrounding them just tossed them back with their buddies. Ride with a dumbass, die with a dumbass.

By the time she'd finished, she'd nearly hacked his head off. When I knew he was dead, I pulled Annie off him, careful to keep hold of the hand holding the knife so I didn't get stabbed. Rocket grabbed the knife and I moved away from the carnage with Annie in my arms.

I took her straight to the water and went until the water lapped at my upper thighs. I didn't want to get too far out or stay in the water too long in case any curious sharks were in the area, but I had to get the blood off her as best I could.

Her cries rang out all around us, the wind carrying the sound out to sea. I let her rage while I washed her. Once I was headed back to shore, I palmed the back of her head and pressed her face to my neck.

"Scream all you want now, baby. Scream into my skin and let me have it."

She sobbed like her heart was breaking. And maybe it was. She had a lot to work through, but I was going to be there for her. All of us were. Because we were a family.

I carried her to the clubhouse and to the room I'd

taken for us while we were in the city. We went straight to the shower where I adjusted the water, stripped her bare, then climbed in the stall with her.

I held her tightly for a long time. Hot water cascaded over us in a gentle flow. Annie continued to cry, but it wasn't the heart-wrenching wailing that it had been on the beach. I had no idea what that bastard had done to her. She hadn't told me specifics because she said she wasn't ready to relive it. I now knew that whatever she'd experienced had been pretty fucking bad.

When the water started to cool and the storm of grief and horror had passed, I dried Annie carefully and took her to bed. She'd pulled me down to press her into the mattress and kissed me like she was starving for my touch.

"Dominic," she whimpered as I kissed my way down her neck to lick a path down the center of her chest. "Oh, God! What are you doing?"

I continued until I got to her mound. Then I took a long, slow lick from her opening to her clit. Annie screamed, her body convulsing off the bed. I had to fight to hold onto her. She was always like this when I ate her out. Today seemed doubly so. She was wound so tight if she didn't release all that emotion inside her, she'd shatter.

She wrapped her legs around my head to hold me to her. She shimmied over my mouth until she got friction where she needed it, then rode my face with quick snaps of her hips. Annie would never cease to amaze me how she embraced sex as easily as she had, especially given everything she'd gone through. I thought she used it as an outlet because of the pleasure the desperation brought her. It was something we'd have to work on, but we would do it together.

"Mmm…" I hummed against her clit before flicking it with my tongue over and over. Annie's breathing came deep and fast and her body tensed around me.

Before she could come, I shoved her legs apart and crawled up her body. She sobbed in despair as she reached for me, pulling me to her once again.

"Please don't leave me like this, Dom. Please."

"You know I'd never do that, baby. I've got you." I guided my cock to her entrance. She was wet and slick, her folds swollen and hot. I slid inside her with ease.

She closed her eyes tight and let out a long, shuddering breath. "Oh God," she moaned. It was the tone of complete satisfaction. I was giving her what she wanted and she responded beautifully.

I kissed her, thrusting my tongue deep into her mouth. I moved in her, the delicious way her pussy tightened around me testing my control. She was tight and hot, clenching around me in a way that threatened to make me come before I was ready. I wanted to take it slow, give her the time she needed, but Annie had other ideas.

She immediately began to rock against me, meeting each of my thrusts with thrusts of her own. Soon enough, we were in perfect sync. The sounds of pleasure we both made became louder as my pace quickened. I was just as affected as she was, completely lost in the beautiful, courageous woman in my arms.

Annie cried out as she climaxed first, her body rigid beneath mine as she quivered and gasped for air. I waited until she'd ridden out the orgasm as far as she could and started to float back to earth before I followed her over the edge. I came inside her with a groan that rumbled through my chest.

Breathing hard, sweat beading over my skin, I collapsed on top of Annie, wrapping my arms tightly around her and rolling us to our sides. Sweat coated our bodies, cooling us as the warm, humid night air filtered through the open window to dry our skin as we recovered.

I held her close till she fell into a restless sleep. In the morning, we would deal with the aftermath of the fight. I'd check in with Rocket in a few minutes, but all I wanted was to hold my girl. Annie was mine. Forever. *Mine*. Rocket would let me know if there was anything that needed my immediate attention. He saw what happened and knew I'd need some time to take care of Annie. I had her with me, wrapped safely in my arms. Tomorrow, we'd head back home. Once I had her safely locked behind the walls of our compound, I'd breathe easier. I wanted Annie locked away and away from the reach of anyone or anything that meant her harm.

For now, though, we both needed rest. I had her with me. She was safe. In my arms, and that was all that mattered.

Epilogue
Dom

By the time I got Annie back home the next morning, Rocket had taken care of the prisoners. There had been no reason to interrogate. Venus and Piston had taken a couple of the Salvation's Bane members to the Grace of the Divine camp. Apparently, Venus and Piston and they'd taken it from there.

What they found there must have been pretty bad because, to my understanding, the guys burnt the camp to the ground and brought home any child under eighteen who wanted to come. They'd all come there with parents who were either too far gone in the cult to care about their children, or had died along the way. If Ringo had it right, more of them were orphaned than had parents left in that God awful place. Grim Road and Salvation's Bane both gained several young women, all of whom had been horribly abused. Most of it was mental and sexual. The men of the cult had been careful not to leave obvious signs of abuse where anyone could see. I had yet to meet any of the women, but, once Annie had time to come to terms with everything that had happened, we'd meet them together.

We'd only been home a few hours. All of it had been spent in bed. Annie acknowledged she needed to tell me the rest of what had happened, but not today. I agreed with her.

"If you're waiting for what I did to hit me, it already did. And you know what?"

"What's that, honey?"

"It was gross. And I hate blood." She sighed, rubbing her cheek over my chest. "But I don't regret one single part of it. I snapped and the timing could probably have been better, but he needed to die. I was happy to send him straight to hell."

"That's my girl."

She actually giggled. "I can't believe you're actually proud I killed someone."

"We're going to see the women Venus and Lemon brought back here tomorrow. These are women who lived through at least some of what you did. Do you think they'd agree with me?"

She snorted derisively. "Yeah. They'd agree. At least, most of them would. There were some who were treated better, but I think it was actually worse for them. They were usually one of that bastard's 'wives'." She made air quotes. "I don't remember ever living anywhere else other than the camp until Venus brought me here. But one thing I've learned in the real world is that when a man takes a woman, he protects her. He doesn't terrorize her or berate her." She snuggled closer to me and gripped my bare shoulder with her fingers, clinging so sweetly to me. "At least, none of you guys do. From what I saw at Salvation's Bane, they're the same way. The men are really protective of their women and children."

"It's not always that way, but for us it is." I shrugged. "I always figure, if a man won't protect the people who are supposed to matter most to him, how can you trust him to have your back?"

"Not bad insight." She stretched, brushing her breasts against my chest where she was sprawled half on top of me.

"Can I ask you something?" There was one question I wanted to have an answer for. It wasn't important, but I was curious.

"Anything." She sounded sated and sleepy and I really liked that sound.

"When did you learn Mandarin?"

She shrugged. "I'm really good at languages. I'd already learned a lot just by being in the camp. I could already translate some of what he was saying, but, apparently, Mandarin isn't always what it appears. Even the way a person inflects a syllable can make a difference in what they mean. The at home course I found said it was the most difficult language to learn. After my crash course, I agree."

"So you put the pieces together after leaving the camp."

"Something like that. It made things make a lot more sense."

Annie's thigh was bent, resting on my own leg. She slid it higher until she did a lazy roll and moved to straddle my hips. Since the first time we'd had sex, Annie had become more aggressive, demanding her pleasure. I was only too happy to give her what she wanted. Reaching between us, Annie guided my rapidly hardening cock inside her wet pussy.

"I need you, Dominic." Her whimper was full of desire, but also a promise that I could lose myself in her body.

"You have me, baby. Tell me what you want."

"You to fuck me. Make me come."

I slid my hands around her torso to rest them flat on her back. She rose and fell on my cock, riding me with sensuous thrusts of her hips. I loved the way she rocked against me, the way she moved and moaned in pleasure as we fucked. She was like no other woman I'd ever been with. Uninhibited, passionate, fierce. Fucking my girl felt like the greatest thing in the fucking world and I wanted never wanted this to end.

"Look at me," I commanded softly.

Annie looked down at me, her eyes blazing with

lust. "Do you love me?"

I didn't even hesitate because my answer was always the same and I never tired of saying it. "More than anything."

She smiled before closing her eyes once more and surrendering to the demands of her body. She shuddered, her muscles rippling as she tried to match my rhythm. It was sexy as hell and did funny things to me because it meant she wasn't just accepting me, she was just as desperate for me as I was for her.

"Harder," she demanded on a small whimper, her words trembling with need.

I obliged, slamming up into her with a growl before rolling us so she was on her back with me over her, and I started to fuck her in earnest.

Annie arched her back, crying out in ecstasy as we found our pace together once more. I could feel my orgasm building but didn't want to come yet. Not until Annie did.

When she started shuddering beneath me, the first telltale signs of her approaching orgasm, I slid one hand up to cup her breast. She cried out again, bucking against me as she came hard on a second strangled scream. Her pussy pulsed around me, pushing me straight toward what I knew would be a mind-numbing orgasm.

Sure enough, my own release followed quickly after hers. I groaned out her name, wrapping my arms tightly around her once more as I rode out the pleasure, pumping her full of my hot, sticky cum. It was disappointing knowing that seed could never take root, but I had the feeling we'd have our hands full with the young women new to our home.

We lay together in a heap on the bed once more, panting for breath. Annie's face was buried in my neck, her breath warm against my skin. The room settled into a soft silence. I stroked her hair gently, the silky strands slipping through my fingers in a mesmerizing rasp.

Outside, the compound was quiet too. Rocket and the others knew not to disturb us unless absolutely necessary. This was our time to heal after everything that had happened.

I kissed her forehead softly, pride swelling in my chest for the incredible woman she had become. Injured and scarred but never broken. She was a survivor, my fierce warrior queen.

"I'm not always gonna be the most demonstrative person, Annie. But I want you to know that I love you."

She still had her eyes closed, but her lips lifted in a drowsy smile. "I love you too, Dom."

"You know, I told you once to call me Dom. Everyone else does."

"Yeah. You did." She was still smiling, but didn't open her eyes.

"Well, I think I changed my mind. I like it when you call me Dominic."

"I can do that."

I took a breath because admitting this second part wasn't going to be easy, but it had to be done. "Also, I was wrong."

She was silent for a long moment, her brows knit together in confusion even though she still didn't open her eyes. I think I'd finally worn her out. "You're gonna have to explain that one." She shrugged. "I mean, you could be referring to anything."

Took me a second, but I finally realized she'd nailed a put-down spectacularly. "You little brat!" So I tickled her.

Annie squealed, thrashing and laughing in my arms until I finally relented. Her smile was glorious. I remembered the first time I'd seen her in the stupid bikini contest. She'd been beautiful and exotic, but a shell of the woman she was turning into now. She just needed someone to give a shit about her, someone to have her back. That was me.

"Yeah, baby. I was wrong. About Tina being my one true love."

She gasped, her eyes going wide. "Dominic," she whispered my name and I could see the hope in her eyes and knew I was making the right decision. Not because it was what she obviously wanted, but because I now knew that, while I might have loved Tina, it was a pale shadow next to what I felt for Annie.

"It's you, Annie." I tried to inject as much love and respect and admiration in my words as I could. Because Annie had told me she thought of me as her hero, but the fact was, she was mine. "It will always be you."

As I watched, Annie's eyes welled with tears. Two streaked down her temples, but she gave me a watery smile. "It'll always be you for me too, Dominic."

"I love you, baby. Be my old lady."

She laughed and cried at the same time, sliding her hand up to cup my cheek. "I love you too. And I'll be proud to be your old lady."

Things weren't perfect, and I was sure there would be some bumps along the way, but I also knew we were stronger together than we ever were apart. No matter what lay ahead for us, we would conquer it. Together.

Marteeka Karland

International bestselling author Marteeka Karland leads a double life as an action romance writer by evening and a semi-domesticated housewife by day. Known for her down-and-dirty MC romances, Marteeka takes pleasure in spinning tales of tenacious, protective heroes and spirited heroines. She staunchly advocates that every character deserves a blissful ending.

Marteeka finds joy in baking, and gardening with her husband. Make sure to visit her website to stay updated with her most recent projects. Don't forget to register for her newsletter which will pepper you with a potpourri of Teeka's beloved recipes, book suggestions, autograph events, and a plethora of interesting tidbits.

Marteeka at Changeling: changelingpress.com/marteeka-karland-a-39

Want more?
Teeka's Dark Erotica side: Wanda Violet O.
changelingpress.com/wanda-violet-o-a-226

Bones MC Multiverse

Bones MC
Shadow Demons
Salvation's Bane MC
Black Reign MC
Iron Tzars MC
Grim Road MC
Bones MC Legends
Bones MC Audio
Salvation's Bane MC Audio
Iron Tzars MC Audio
Bones MC Print Duets

Changeling Press LLC

Contemporary Action Adventure, Sci-Fi, Steampunk, Dark Fantasy, Urban Fantasy, Paranormal, and BDSM Romance available in e-book, audio, and print format at ChangelingPress.com -- MC Romance, Werewolves, Vampires, Dragons, Shapeshifters and Horror -- Tales from the edge of your imagination.

Where can I get Changeling Press Books?

Changeling Press e-books are available at ChangelingPress.com, Amazon, Apple Books, Barnes & Noble, Kobo, Smashwords, and other online retailers, including Everand Subscription and Kobo Subscription Services. Print books are available at Amazon, Barnes and Noble, and by ISBN special order through your local bookstores.

Changeling Press, LLC

ChangelingPress.com

www.ingramcontent.com/pod-product-compliance
Lightning Source LLC
Chambersburg PA
CBHW070444260626

47161CB00004B/1201